喚醒你的英文語感！

Get a Feel for English !

喚醒你的英文語感！

Get a Feel for English !

# Writing Argumentative Essays in English

# 論證型
# 英文寫作
# 速成教戰

升‧留學
學術報告
頂尖致勝！

作者 Quentin Brand

Apex

Precision analysis

歸納考題

Organizing ideas

組織想法

Critical thinking

批判思辨

Error analysis

分析範例

貝塔｜語測
檢測學習平台
高點 美語系列

# CONTENTS 目錄

# 前言

你可能需要為雅思、托福、GRE、GEPT 或學士後醫學系的入學考試寫一篇英文作文,本書以學士後醫學系的寫作考題為範例,目的是盡可能以簡單的方式幫助你學會寫出一篇文章,同時讓你的寫作得到最佳結果。這些語言技巧和寫作策略都是基於筆者多年來為各類應試者教授寫作的經驗,希望藉此幫助所有考生和所有讀者成功克服各種寫作困難點,在各項測驗中得到更高的分數。

在開始學習寫作之前,我要向大家介紹 Leximodel,這是我看待語言的方式,也是貫穿本書各章節學習內容的重要觀念,請務必要詳讀並且徹底理解。

## ▌語言是由字串所構成 (the Leximodel)

leximodel 是我看待語言的方式,它是以一個很簡單的概念為基礎:

**Language consists of words which are used with other words.**
語言是由字串所構成的。

這個看法非常簡單易懂。它的意思是:與其把語言看成文法和單字,與其學習個別的單字,然後再學習句型,我們認為語言是一群字或是字的組合,即語言是由字串所構成。

也就是說,有些字的組合比其他字的組合更容易預測。例如,我們可以預測到 listen 的後面永遠都會跟著 to,而不是 at 或 under 之類的其他字,

所以我們可以說這個組合是完全固定的 (fixed)。另一方面，English 這個單字後面可接很多字，例如 gentleman、test、tea，所以很難預測接下來是哪一個字。我們可以說，這種組合是不固定的，它是流動的 (fluid)。

我們可以根據可預測度，把這些字串組合沿著以下的光譜來擺放：

**The Spectrum of Predictability**

← **listen to** ——————————————— **English test** →
　　fixed　　　　　　　　　　　　　　　　　 fluid

知道哪些字串組合是固定的，哪些是不固定的，可以讓你更快學習和使用英文。如果你學習的是一群字，而不是單一一個字，你的學習速度會更快，也會知道如何使用它們，因為這些字從來都不是單獨使用的。

我們可以把所有字串（稱之為 MWIs = multi word items）分為三類：chunks、set-phrases 和 word partnerships。由於中文裡沒有和這些詞相對應的概念，所以請直接記住它們的英文。讓我們更仔細看這三類字串，你很快就會知道，它們其實很容易理解和使用。

### ⊡ Chunks

chunks 通常被我們當成文法的部分。chunks 通常很短，並且由 meaning words（有意義的字，如 listen、depend）和 function words（功能性的字，如 to、on）所組成。chunks 包含了不固定元素和固定元素。例如，我們可以改變動詞時態 (was listening to / have not been listening to)，但不能改變後面的 to 這個字。

你知道的 chunks 可能已經很多，卻不知道自己知道！我們來進行一個任務，看看你是否明白我的意思。進行這個任務時，很重要的是不要先看答案，所以，請不要作弊！

A chunk is a combination of words which is more or less fixed. Every time a word in the chunk is used, it must be used with its partner(s). Chunks combine fixed and fluid elements of language. When you learn a new word, you should learn the chunk. There are thousands of chunks in English. One way you can help yourself to improve your English is by noticing and keeping a database of the chunks you find as you read. You should also try to memorize as many as possible.

現在，請把你的答案和下列語庫做比較。如果你沒有找到那麼多的 chunks，請再看看你能不能找到語庫裡所有的 chunks。

| | |
|---|---|
| … a combination of n.p. … | … thousands of n.p. … |
| … more or less … | … in English … |
| … every time v.p. … | … help yourself to V … |
| … be used with n.p. … | … keep a database of n.p. … |
| … combine s/th and s/th. … | … try to V … |
| … elements of n.p. … | … as many as possible … |

- 注意，語庫中的 chunks 是用原形 be 來表示 be 動詞，而不是 is 或 are。
- 記錄 chunks 時，會在 chunks 的前後都加上 …（刪節號）。
- 注意，有些 chunks 的後面會接著 V、Ving、n.p.（noun phrase，名詞片語）或 v.p.（verb phrase，動詞片語）。關於這部分，你很快就會學到更多。
- 學習大量的 chunks 可以提升在寫作上的文法精準度。你將在這本書學到很多 chunks。

## ➡ Set-phrases

set-phrases 通常被當成組織或互動的部分。我們用 set-phrases 來完成工作，例如在餐廳點餐、在文章裡組織訊息。因為我們平常都用一樣的用

語來做這些常見的事，所以 set-phrases 是更固定的 chunks。它們通常比較長，而且可能包含好幾個 chunks。chunks 通常是沒頭沒尾的片斷文字組合；set-phrases 通常有個開頭或結尾，或是兩者都有，這表示有時候一個完整的句子也可能是一組 set-phrase。現在請看看下面的語庫並進行任務。

**✐ Task 2** 請想想以下的 **set-phrases** 你是否曾在哪裡見過？把認識的打勾。

- [ ] I disagree with the view that v.p. …
- [ ] There are many reasons why I think so.
- [ ] I do not believe that v.p. …
- [ ] It's my opinion that v.p. …
- [ ] There are many ways to solve this problem.
- [ ] I (dis)agree with this, and think that v.p. …
- [ ] This essay will look at some of the common problems and will then suggest two solutions.
- [ ] I can think of two solutions to this problem.
- [ ] There are two/three main reasons.
- [ ] I firmly believe that v.p. …
- [ ] There's no doubt in my mind that v.p. …

- 注意，set-phrases 通常以大寫字母開頭，或用句點結束。這三個點 (...) 表示句子裡不固定的部分要開始了。
- 你可能已經在許多文章中看過這些 set-phrases。它們通常用來表達對一個議題的看法。
- 由於 set-phrases 是三類字串中最固定的一種，所以在學習時，必須非常仔細留意每個 set-phrases 的細節。稍後對此會有更詳細的說明。
- 有些 set-phrases 以 n.p. 結尾，有些以 v.p. 結尾。
- 學習大量的 set-phrases 可以彰顯你在寫作上組織想法的能力。在本書中將可學到很多 set-phrases。

## ⇥ Word partnerships

　　word partnerships 是三類字串中最不固定，也就是流動性最高的一類。它是由兩個或更多的意義字（不同於 chunks 結合了意義字和功能字）所組成，通常是「動詞 + 形容詞 + 名詞」或是「名詞 + 名詞」的組合。word partnerships 會根據你寫的主題而改變，而 chunks 和 set-phrases 則可用於任何主題。現在，請進行下一個任務，藉此更清楚了解我的意思。

✎ **Task 3** 請看下列各組 **word partnerships**，並判斷它們來自於哪一種主題內容。請從主題列表中選擇。

| 主題 |
|---|
| A. acting and theatre　　　B. psychological experiments<br>C. the environment　　　　D. the history of cities<br>E. the law　　　　　　　　F. the life of whales<br>G. social media |

### word partnerships ①

natural resources / environmental pollution

global warming / carbon dioxide emissions

主題是（　　）

### word partnerships ②

personal responsibility / conduct experiments / analyze results / collect data

主題是（　　）

### word partnerships ③

social networks / social withdrawal / virtual reality game / addictive behavior

主題是（　　）

- 請注意，word partnerships 包含的意義由兩個字組合而成，有時候甚至由三個或四個字組合而成。
- 學習大量 word partnerships 可以讓你精確使用字彙和表達你的想法。

➡ Task 3 答案：① C　② B　③ G

因此，我們最終版的 leximodel，現在看起來是這樣：

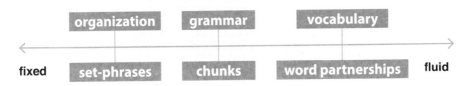

**The Spectrum of Predictability**

這樣更接近語言在人腦中記憶和使用的習慣。如果你把重點放在學習 chunks，你的文法能力會提升，因為大多數的文法錯誤實際上是誤用了 chunks；如果你把重點放在學習 set-phrases，組織文章的能力會提升；而若是把重點放在 word partnerships，則使用詞彙的精準度會更高。

# ▋如何使用這本書

現在，我想各位應該會認為 leximodel 似乎是個不錯的概念，但可能還是有些疑問。讓我來歸納一下你可能會有的疑問是哪些，並看看能否幫忙解答。

問 **請問這本書如何使用 Leximodel？**
答 本書會呈現出語言裡所有最常出現的固定部分（chunks、set-phrases 和 word partnerships，但大部分是 set-phrases 和 chunks），書中將告訴你如何學習並在英文寫作中使用它們。

問 **有沒有什麼問題是我需要注意的？**
答 有。這本書裡有許多練習，是設計用來幫你解決一些問題。學習 set-phrases 和 chunks 的主要問題是：

> **You must focus on the details of the set-phrase or chunk.**
> 你必須把重點放在 set-phrase 或 chunk 的細節上。

在學習或使用 set-phrases 和 chunks 的時候，有四個部分的細節必須特別注意。

1. **小詞**（像是 a、the、to、in、at、on、and、but 之類的字）。這些字都非常難記，但難記還只是問題的一部分。如果你誤用了小詞，將會改變 set-phrase 或 chunk，而改變它們就表示出錯了。

2. **字尾**（有些字的字尾是 -ed，有些是 -ing，有些是 -ment，有些是 -s 或沒有 -s）。字尾改變了，字的意思也會隨之改變。如果弄錯字尾，會改變 set-phrase 或 chunk，也就等於是用錯了。

3. **set-phrases 和 chunks 的結尾**。在前面任務一和任務二中看到 set-

phrases 和 chunks 可能以 v.p.、n.p.、V 或 Ving 結尾，我們把這些縮寫稱為 codes。（v.p. = verb phrase 動詞片語；n.p. = noun phrase 名詞片語；V = verb 動詞，以及 Ving = Ving 動名詞。）稍後將學習到更多這方面的知識。

把 set-phrase 和 chunk 加入句子之中時，可能出現許多錯誤。當你在學習 setphrase 或 chunk 時，也請學習 code。弄錯 code 會改變 set-phrase 和 chunk，等於是寫錯了。

4. **完整的 set-phrase 或 chunk**。你必須確定自己已學到並使用完整的 set-phrase 或 chunk。所以實際上，我們可以說 1、2 和 3 的錯誤，也同時是 4 的錯誤。對吧？

問 你會如何協助我？

答 我在後面許多單元設計了許多練習，讓你學習正確使用 set-phrase 和 chunk。你會進行一系列不同類型的練習，例如注意錯誤、注意 n.p 和 v.p. 之間的差異、訂正錯誤，並且根據 set-phrases 的意義將它們分門別類。所有這些練習，都是設計用來幫助你學習和記憶新的用語。我會給你正確的答案和詳盡的解析。另外，我會用範例文章告訴你許多正確使用這些用語的例子。也會告訴你，我在台灣教書多年來，看到人們最常誤用的狀況，並且分析到底錯在哪裡。

問 我該做些什麼？

答 你應該要確保自己徹底完成每一個單元。這些單元都經過精心設計，目的是幫助你學習，所以你不應該跳過任何單元、任何練習，或是在還沒完成練習前就直接看答案。請務必從頭到尾徹底學習所有單元，並利用每個單元最後的清單幫你追蹤自己的學習狀況。

問 我如何得到回饋？

答 你可能會認為，除非有人給你回饋，否則練習寫文章的幫助不大。在某

個程度上來說，這樣想是對的。但是，根據我實際的經驗來說，就算你沒有機會得到別人的回饋，盡可能多練習依然是非常關鍵的。你在本書學到的用語和思考方式，會幫助你的大腦記憶它們。

**問** 你還有其他祕訣可以教我嗎？

**答** 有。多閱讀。所有研究都清楚顯示，不管參加什麼考試，英文閱讀量較大的學生，分數都比較高，所以每天盡量多讀英文。大量閱讀可以讓你讀到更多字彙，並幫助你學會它們，日積月累下來，英文的聽說讀寫能力必能有所提升。

所以，你準備好要開始了嗎？

*Quentin Brand*

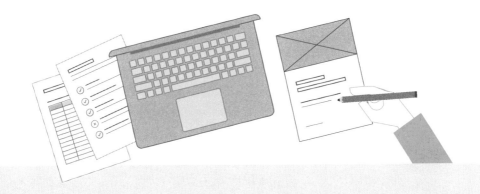

# Unit 1
## 如何以英文來組織資訊
**How to Organise Information in English**

在寫作的過程中，經由腦力激盪對主題產生想法固然很重要，但是如何將想法有邏輯地組織起來更是一門大學問。尤其在英文寫作測驗時，能夠根據英文這個語言特定的模式來組織自己的想法，更是獲取高分的首要條件，千萬不可以想到什麼就寫什麼。

在英文裡，所有資訊都要根據基本的結構組織起來。這個基本結構是：

**general ideas come first, followed by specific examples**
先寫概括想法，再寫特定、具體例子

general ideas「概括想法」和 specific ideas「特定想法」之間，永遠都有一條明顯的差異和界線。這個結構非常重要，重要到文法和字彙也是用這種方式組織。中文的組織結構則很不一樣。在中文，概括和特定之間的差異並不重要，所以它們的界線並不清楚。舉一個最簡單的例子，中文裡的名詞並不會因為東西是一個或多個而產生變化，但是在英文裡會在字的後面加上 s 來表示複數，沒有 s 則表示一般概括性的事物。再看一個例子：

**Doctors are usually overworked.** → 是概指一般的醫生（複數）。
這句話並沒有指是哪一個特定的醫生，所以我們知道它說的是一般所有的醫生。

**The doctor is overworked.** → 是指某個特定的醫生。
我們可以從句子前後的語言和脈絡，知道句中說的是指哪一個特定的醫生。

你必須提升對英文這個重要部分的敏感度。為了幫助你清楚了解概括資訊與特定資訊的差別，我們要進行幾個任務。

### Task 1
**請將以下文字按照你所觀察到的原則進行組織。**

| orange | green | colour | blue | yellow | purple |
|--------|-------|--------|------|--------|--------|
| car | truck | motorbike | vehicle | bus | coach |
| table | chair | furniture | bed | closet | bench |

解答・說明

☆ 希望你能看出來，把文字組織起來的最好方式是這樣：colour 是概括性概念，orange、green、blue、yellow、purple 是特定的例子；vehicle 是概括性概念，car、truck、motorbike、bus、coach 是特定的例子；furniture 是概括性概念，table、chair、bed、closet、bench 是特定的例子。另一個表達方式則是 orange、green、blue、yellow 和 purple 是顏色的種類等等，以此類推。

☆ 這裡很重要的是能看出這些單字之間的 general-specific 關係：vehicle、colour、furniture 是 general，其他的單字則是這些一般概念的 specific 例子。

　　請用更複雜的資訊再嘗試練習一遍。

## ✏ Task 2

請將以下文字分類。注意，你須判斷出有哪些類別，以及有多少字。

| | | | |
|---|---|---|---|
| Africa | cat | in | organ |
| after | composer | kidney | pear |
| apple | continent | lawyer | preposition |
| Asia | dog | lung | professional |
| at | doctor | mammal | Scarlatti |
| Bach | fruit | monarchy | tyranny |
| brain | government | monarchy | Beethoven |
| architect | horse | Europe | democracy |
| | | orange | |

解答・說明

請參考以下表格檢查你的答案，並且閱讀我的說明。

| general | specific |
|---|---|
| mammal | horse / dog / cat |
| composer | Bach / Beethoven / Scarlatti |

| fruit | apple / orange / pear |
|---|---|
| preposition | after / in / at |
| continent | Asia / North Africa |
| government | democracy / monarchy / tyranny |
| professional | architect / doctor / lawyer |
| organ | lung / kidney / brain |

☆ 希望你可以看出這些字被組織成概括想法和具體例子。例如 horse、dog 和 cat 是 mammal 的例子。

至此，你應該很清楚概括和特定的概念，接著就來看看該如何運用這個知識寫出一個段落。

英文裡的段落通常先有概括性的陳述。這個概括性的陳述叫做主題句 (topic sentence)。主題句是用來告訴讀者這個段落的大意，之後，會有更多具體的資訊——通常是三個或四個句子——來支撐這個概括性的陳述。請看下圖。

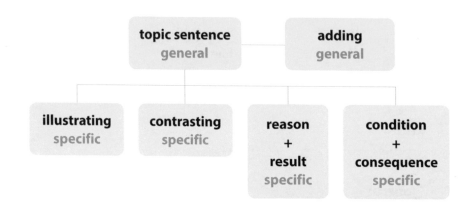

　　請注意，主題句之所以是主題句，並不是因為它是第一個句子，而是因為它含有最概括性的資訊。其他句子則都跟著主題句，而且其他句子之所以有意義，是因為它們都以某種方式指涉主題句。也就是說，如果我們把主題句從段落中剔除，就很難清楚說明其他句子指涉的對象是誰，以及這個段落大致上在說些什麼。我們來進行一個任務，讓你可以更了解我的意思。

## Task 3

請從下方文句清單選擇一個合適的主題句，以完成段落。

_____. There are three main types of tax. The first is personal income tax, which is tax charged on the money which people earn from their jobs. Another kind of tax is corporation tax, which is a tax paid by businesses and corporations on the profits they make each year. Then there is value added tax, or sales tax, which is a tax paid by someone buying goods or services. This kind of tax is usually a percentage of the total cost of the purchased goods or services.

A  A filibuster is the process of delaying or preventing the passing or making of a new law by extending the discussion time about the new law and thus delaying the vote on the new law.

B  In recent years, the destruction of the rainforests in South East Asia and the Amazon basin has been increasing.

C  Microcredit, also known as microfinance, is the lending of money to poor people who live in the countryside, especially in developing countries.

D  Taxation is how the state raises money from its citizens to pay for the services the state offers to its citizens, and to pay for the costs of government.

E  Volcanoes are places where magma, which is a kind of melted rock below the earth's surface, pushes through to the surface of the earth in an eruption, or explosion.

課稅是指國家向其國民收取款項，以支應國家為國民提供服務以及政府運作成本的方式。稅賦主要有三類。首先是個人所得稅，依民眾從工作中所賺得的金額來課稅。另一種稅是公司稅，指事業和公司依每年獲利所繳納的稅。然後是增值稅或營業稅，即購買商品或服務的人所繳納的稅，這種稅通常是商品或服務購入總成本的某個百分比。

A 拖延戰術是把對新法的討論時間拉長，因而延緩對新法的表決，以延緩或阻止新法通過或制訂。

B 近年來，東南亞和亞馬遜流域的雨林所遭到的破壞有增無減。

C 微型信貸又稱微型金融，是把錢放貸給住在鄉村的窮人，尤其是在開發中國家。

D 課稅是指國家向其國民收取款項，以支應國家為國民提供服務以及政府運作成本的方式。

E 岩漿是一種地表下的熔岩，噴發或爆炸時衝出地表的地方即為火山。

☆ 最適合這個段落的主題句是第 D. 句。你也許有答對，因為 tax 這個字不斷出現在段落中。

☆ Taxation 是個概括性的字，意思是徵稅的過程；Tax 則是個具體的字眼。這裡的主題句說的是一般的徵稅，其他的句子則都說明具體的徵稅種類，就像 colour 是概括性的字眼，blue 則是顏色的一種。

☆ 所以，主題句之所以是主題句，是因為它含有最概括性的資訊，而不是因為它是第一個句子。實際上，主題句經常出現在段落的中間，或有時候出現在段落的後半段，但讀者之所以知道那是主題句，靠的不是它的位置，而是因為它和其他句子的概括性關係。

☆ 然而，在你的短文中，你應該把主題句放在文章段落的開頭。

　　我們再來進行另一個任務，把這部分釐清。

**Task 4**

請將句子正確排列。哪一句是主題句？

---

A  Corpus linguistics is useful because it allows researchers to study huge amounts of language very quickly.

B  Corpus linguistics is the term used to describe the analysis of language using computers.

C  In order to do corpus linguistics, or computational language research, you need two things: a large body of language, called a corpus, and a software program called a concordancer.

D  The bigger the corpus is, the more useful it is for this kind of research.

E  The concordancer can search through the corpus very quickly to find examples of language use the researcher is interested in.

F  The corpus is stored electronically on a computer and includes all kinds of samples of spoken and written language.

---

| 主題句 | _____ | | 第四句 | _____ |
| 第二句 | _____ | | 第五句 | _____ |
| 第三句 | _____ | | 第六句 | _____ |

中譯‧解答‧說明

主題句：**B** 譯 語料庫語言學是為了描述用電腦來分析詞語而使用的專有名詞。

第二句：**C** 譯 如果要做語料庫語言學或是運算式的語言研究，你需要兩樣東西：大量的詞語，就是所謂的語料庫，以及軟體程式，就是所謂的詞語檢索工具。

第三句：**F** 譯 語料庫是以電子化的方式儲存在電腦裡，包括了口說和書寫詞語的各種範例。

第四句：**D** 譯 語料庫愈大，對這種研究就愈有用。

第五句：**E** 譯 詞語檢索功能可非常迅速地搜尋語料庫，以針對研究人員感興趣的詞語用法去尋找例子。

第六句：A 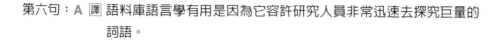 語料庫語言學有用是因為它容許研究人員非常迅速去探究巨量的詞語。

☆ 首先，不用擔心自己看不懂句子中的字彙。你不是非得要知道這些字彙的意思才能了解到概括／特定的形態，而這才是我要你在此去聚焦的事。

☆ B 是主題句，因為它是最概括的句子：它介紹和說明 corpus linguistics「語料庫語言學」這個專有名詞。其他的句子則提供了更多語料庫語言學的具體資訊。

☆ C 是下一個句子，因為它告訴我們 corpus linguistics 更具體的細節：我們需要的兩個東西。接著，F 是下一句，因為 corpus 是 C 句提到的第一個詞，而 D 句用更具體的細節說明 F 句。C 句的第二個詞是 concordancer，這個詞在 E 句有更多具體的說明和解釋。

☆ 最後，整個段落是用 A 句來總結。亦即不先讀遍其他的資訊，我們就不會了解語料庫語言學為什麼有用。

☆ 另一方面，也許你會把 A 視為第二句，因為它較為概括。這樣做也可以。

☆ 主要的重點在於，你必須開始從 general/specific 的角度來進行思考。如果你了解這點，那就太棒了！


　　在你結束這個單元之前，請將下列的清單看過，確定你能將所有要點都勾選起來。如果有一些要點你還搞不清楚，請回頭再次研讀本單元的相關部分。


　　□ 我學到了如何以英文來組織資訊。
　　□ 我學到了把概括資訊和特定資訊區分清楚的重要性。
　　□ 我學到了主題句是段落裡最概括的資訊。
　　□ 我了解段落是如何圍繞著主題句來組織。
　　□ 我已經練習了把段落組織起來。

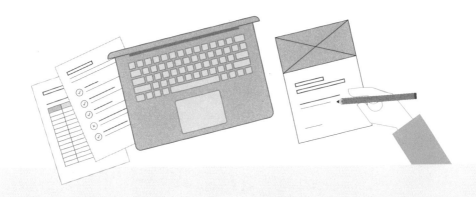

# Unit 2

## 如何分析題目
### How to Analyse the Title

在本單元裡,你將學習如何去分析題目,也會做很多這方面的練習。練習很重要,不該把它跳過,因為透過大量的分析題目練習,能幫助你在考試時更快速、輕鬆地完成這件事,不但節省時間,也會讓你更有自信地進行接下來的寫作。

在大多數英文寫作測驗中，你可能會被要求寫的文章有兩種類型：problem/solution「問題／解決方法」的文章，以及 argument/opinion「論證／意見」的文章。在第一類型文章中，你必須依提示詳細地描述問題，並且提出一些該如何解決問題的建議。在「論證／意見」的文章中，你則必須針對一個主題表達自己的意見，然後提出論證來支持你的意見。

題目的提示有兩個部分。

1. 一段陳述。此陳述可能有兩種形式：「描述問題」或「一個觀點」。

> **描述問題**
>
> Global warming has recently become the most urgent long-term issue the world faces, and many people think not enough is being done to solve this problem.

在這個問題／解決方法的範例中，你可以看到對某個問題的描述，以及像是 issue、problem、situation 等單字。

> **觀點**
>
> In recent years, many countries have become extremely concerned about the increase in crimes against immigrants. Better enforcement of the law and stricter punishments are necessary.

在這個觀點的範例中，你可以看到第一個句子描述了某一個狀況，第二個句子則針對該狀況提出一個觀點。

2. 一個指示。

問題

What problems are the effects of global warming causing us now, and what can we do to solve them?

在問題的情況中，你必須針對該問題舉出更多的例子，然後建議解決的辦法。

觀點

Write an essay expressing your point of view.

在觀點的情況下，你必須同意或反對該觀點，並提出論述以表達反對或支持它的原因。

　　這兩類題目都要求你透過論證來說服他人。其中很重要的是，你必須知道題目要求你寫的是哪一種類型的文章，因為各類文章所要求的組織類型不同，詞語也不同。為了幫助你了解這一點，我們要進行一些練習，把重點放在題目的說明文字上。

## ✏ Task 1

**請閱讀這些常見的說明文字，並將它們分類放進下方的表格中。**

• Discuss both of these views and give your own opinion.
• Discuss possible ways of Ving….
• Discuss the advantages and disadvantages of this.
• Do you believe that v.p. …?
• How do you think v.p. …?
• Identify the problems and suggest ways to V….
• To what extent do you agree or disagree?
• What are some ways to V…?
• What can governments do to V...?
• What should be done to V…?

- Which do you consider to be the best n.p. ...?
- Write an essay expressing your point of view.

| problem/solution | argument/opinion |
|---|---|
|  |  |

解答．說明

請研讀表格所做的分類，並且閱讀下方說明。

| problem/solution | argument/opinion |
|---|---|
| • How do you think v.p. ...?<br>　對於 v.p.，你認為如何？<br>• What should be done to V...?<br>　如果要 V，應該要怎麼做？<br>• Discuss possible ways of Ving....<br>　針對 Ving 來討論可能的方式。<br>• Identify the problems and suggest<br>　ways to V....<br>　指出問題並建議作法來 V。<br>• What are some ways to V...?<br>　要 V 的一些方法是什麼？<br>• What can governments do to V...?<br>　政府能做什麼來 V？ | • To what extent do you agree or disagree?<br>　你是贊同或不贊同到什麼程度？<br>• Write an essay expressing your point of view.<br>　寫一篇短文來表達你的觀點。<br>• Do you believe that v.p. ...?<br>　你是否相信 v.p.？<br>• Discuss the advantages and disadvantages<br>　of this.<br>　討論這麼做的優缺點。<br>• Discuss both of these views and give your<br>　own opinion.<br>　討論這兩種觀點並提出自己的意見。<br>• Which do you consider to be the best n.p. ...?<br>　你認為哪個會是最好的 n.p.？ |

☆ 請注意，在 problem/solution 的說明文字中，有許多用語是用來建議作法，例如：ways to, What can X do to, should be done to 等等。另外也需留意 What do you think（你的意見）和 How do you think（你的建議）之間的差異。

☆ 請仔細確認 argument/opinion 的說明文字，題目可能只要你提出觀點，或還要你討論相反意見。事實上，就算只寫一句相反的意見，都應該正反意見並陳。

UNIT
2

　　為了有助於分析題目，你應該先在關鍵字彙底下畫線，然後可以把這些字用在你的文章裡，不過在使用時要確定你知道這些關鍵字彙的意思。雖然這裡不太可能會出現你不知道的字彙，但若真的有不認識的字，就要運用你的常識，並且試著依循脈絡猜出它們的意思。如果文章裡有很多字彙你不懂，這表示你的閱讀量實在不夠。請記得，增加字彙量最好的方法就是盡可能多閱讀。

　　接著，要確定自己知道該做些什麼：是 problem/solution essay 還是 argument/opinion essay。

1. 在 **problem/solution essay** 中，你必須更詳細地描述問題，並且提出一些該如何解決問題的建議。在作答時有一點很重要，就是不能只是鉅細靡遺地描述問題或只是提出解決方法。你必須兩者都要著墨，因為閱卷者會想知道你是否懂得表達問題和解決方法。在後續的單元中將會教你該使用哪些用語來表達。

2. 在 **argument/opinion essay** 中，你須針對一個題目表達自己的意見，並且用好的理由和例子來支持你的意見。我建議提出明確的意見，而不要說：「在某些情況下，A 選項比較好；在其他情況下，B 選項比較好」。重點不在於你是否真的同意或反對，因為沒有人真的在意你的想法，閱卷者只在意你是否能提出論證。此外，你必須闡述問題的另一面，並且說明你不支持的原因。有些 argument/opinion essays 可能會要你討論某件事的優點和缺點，同時表達自己的意見。

　　現在，你知道該如何分析題目，我們就來看一些英文寫作的真題範例。

025

## 📝 Extra Practice Essays

請利用前面學過的重點，練習分析以下作文題目。

### TOPIC 1 111 年學士後西醫（高醫）

**IV. Essay Writing: 20 points**

**Write an essay of at least 200 words in an appropriate style on the following topic.**

What does the phrase "medical ethics" mean? How important are "medical ethics" to doctors and patients? Give specific examples to answer the above-mentioned questions.

### TOPIC 2 111 年學士後中醫（義守）

二、作文題（共 20 分）

According to the International Rescue Committee, a global humanitarian aid group, Russia's invasion of Ukraine has uprooted people on a speed and scale not seen since World War II. According to the statistics from the United Nations, more than 4 million Ukrainians have fled the country. Please write an essay on the issues that refugees may encounter in at least 250 words in English.

　　在你結束這個單元之前，請將下列的清單看過，確定你能將所有要點都勾選起來。如果有一些要點你還搞不清楚，請回頭再次研讀本單元的相關部分。

☐ 我學到了如何分析題目。

☐ 我學到了如何區分「問題／解決方法」文章和「論證／意見」文章的差別。

☐ 我知道自己在各類的文章中必須做些什麼。

☐ 我看到一些實際寫作的真題範例，並已確實練習去分析這些題目。

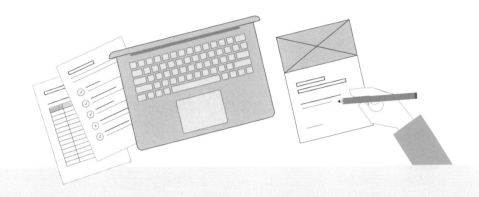

# Unit 3

## 如何規劃回答：
## 問題／解決方法的文章

### How to Plan Your Answer:
### Problem/Solution Essay

在開始寫作前先進行規劃才能有邏輯地組織你的想法，而不是想到什麼就寫什麼。在本單元將說明要怎麼針對「問題／解決方法」的文章來做到這點。

不管你的語言能力有多好，如果沒有把想法組織起來就很難取得高分。意即為了得到高分，你必須表現出你能夠根據特定的模式組織自己的想法，此即我們在 Unit 1 所學到的：general/specific「概括／特定」。

## ★ 透過腦力激盪產生想法

1. 把你腦力激盪出來的想法整理成簡單的表格，這樣可以得到非常基本的結構。我們稍後會練習這部分。
2. 當你在做腦力激盪時，請避免寫完整的句子。相反的，請把重點放在字彙，尤其是搭配字 (word partnerships)，並且把搭配字寫在表格裡正確的欄位。如果字很長，不要把它全部寫出來，只要寫前面一個音節來幫助你記憶即可。盡量多節省一些時間。專心讓想法湧現，然後在它消失之前把它寫下來！
3. 試著幫你的想法思考出一些具體的例子，並且試著為你的建議想出一些結果。
4. 試著平衡你的想法，讓你在「問題／解決方法」的文章裡，有三分之一的問題想法，三分之二的解決想法；以及在「論證／意見」的文章裡，有三分之二的想法支持你的意見，三分之一的想法反駁你的意見。

我們來練習腦力激盪。

### ✎ Task 1

請針對這個題目進行腦力激盪，並把你的想法整理在下方的表格中。

*The destruction of rain forests to create land for agricultural use is a serious problem.*
*What are some of the common problems and what can be done to reduce them?*

| problem | solution |
|---------|----------|
|         |          |

解答・說明

請參考表格內容，並且閱讀下方的說明。

| problem | | solution |
|---------|---|----------|
| • local areas | • flora and fauna | • stop people eating meat all the time |
| • groundcover is burnt | • the loss of | • government–urgently legislate |
| • planet as a whole | | • prevent companies from stripping the land |
| • causes | • terrible air pollution | |
| • impacts | • logging | • enforce the laws – send a message |
| • affects | • soil erosion | |
| • contributes to | • flooding | |
| | • global warming | |
| • loss of wildlife | | |
| • natural habitat | • surrounding countries | |

☆ 針對這個「問題／解決方法」的文章，我把想法大致上組織成兩種類型：problem 和 solution。

☆ 當想法出現在我腦海時，我只是簡短把它寫下來。你可以看到我寫下可以在這篇文章裡使用的動詞：causes, impacts, affects, contributes to，並把它們放在 problem 欄位，但我大概也會在文章裡的 solution 部分使用它們。

☆ 你可以再次看到我沒有寫完整的句子，只是一些搭配字或是片語。

☆ 請注意，我也思考了解決方法的一些結果：enforce the laws–send a message。

☆ 再次提醒，在這個階段時，先不要擔心想法是否有組織。


　　在 Unit 1 裡，你學到了 general「概括」和 specific「特定」的差別，我們來試著把這應用到現在的腦力激盪上。

　　首先要決定哪些字彙是概括性的，把那些字彙變成你的主題句。然後決定要以哪些字彙來為主題句增添特定的資訊。在組織字彙時，要想到文章的最終形式，也就是你認為會需要多少個段落。

　　我用上方 Task 1 的題目來舉例。題目再次如下。

---

*The destruction of rain forests to create land for agricultural use is a serious problem.*

*What are some of the common problems and what can be done to reduce them?*

---

## ✏ Task 2

請研究表格中的 **problem** 欄位，並且閱讀下方的說明。

| problem | |
|---|---|
| A local areas & planet as a whole | A2 flora and fauna |
| B groundcover is burnt | the loss of |
| causes | B1 terrible air pollution |
| impacts | C logging |
| affects | C1 soil erosion |
| contributes to | C2 flooding |
| | D global warming |
| A1 loss of wildlife | |
| A3 natural habitat | B2 surrounding countries |

| solution |
|---|
| stop people eating meat all the time |
| government–urgently legislate |
| prevent companies from stripping the land |
| enforce the laws–send a message |
| all of us |

☆ 我決定要寫兩個大段落當作這篇文章的主體。寫一個段落來說明問題，最後再用一個段落來說明解決方法。

☆ 在這裡，A 句是我的主題句，B、C 和 D 句則是我的支持句。

☆ 我沒有把動詞 causes、impacts、affects、contributes to 和片語 the loss of 標號，因為在這個階段，我還不確定自己會如何用這些詞。我只知道當我寫作時，我會大量使用這些字彙。

現在就來看看當我寫文章時，這樣的規劃會有什麼效果。

## ✏ Task 3

閱讀以下文章的段落並與 Task 2 中的規劃做比對，若字彙是出自 Task 2 表格裡 problem 欄位的就把它畫上底線。

Destroying rainforests causes many problems, not only for the areas where the destruction is taking place, but also for the planet as a whole. In local areas, logging causes loss of wildlife, as many species of flora and fauna lose their natural habitat. When the rainforest is destroyed, the groundcover is often burnt to clear the land quickly. This causes terrible air pollution for the surrounding countries. In addition, the loss of groundcover as a result of logging causes soil erosion, which leads to flooding. Not only this, but rain forest destruction also contributes to global warming.

破壞熱帶雨林會導致許多問題，不僅對發生破壞的地區，而且對整個地球都是如此。在局部地區，伐木會造成野生動物流失，因為很多品種的動植物群失去天然棲地。當熱帶雨林遭到破壞時，地被植物通常會被燒毀以迅速清理土地。這會對周遭國家造成可怕的空氣污染。此外，伐木所衍生出的地被流失會造成土壤侵蝕而導致洪災。不僅如此，破壞雨林還會加劇全球暖化。

☆ 希望你有找到所有的字彙，並且看出我在 Task 2 規劃的結構，如何呈現在最後的段落文章中。

好的，現在換你來試試看。

## ✏ Task 4

**請組織 Task 2 表格 solution 欄位裡的字彙。**

參考答案

請看我如何組織 solution 欄位的字彙，並且將它和下面的段落比較。和之前一樣，請將段落裡的字彙畫上底線。

| problem | |
| --- | --- |
| A local areas & planet as a whole | A2 flora and fauna |
| B groundcover is burnt | the loss of |
| causes<br>impacts<br>affects<br>contributes to | B1 terrible air pollution<br><br>C logging<br>C1 soil erosion<br>C2 flooding |
| A1 loss of wildlife<br>A3 natural habitat | D global warming<br><br>B2 surrounding countries |

| solution |
| --- |
| **B1** stop people eating meat all the time |
| **A** government–urgently legislate |
| **A1** prevent companies from stripping the land |
| **A2** enforce the laws–send a message |
| **B** all of us |

The first solution must come from government. Governments in the countries impacted by this problem must urgently legislate to prevent companies stripping the land. Not only must they legislate, but they must also enforce the laws as well. This will send a message to potential businesses that the law should be obeyed. The second solution must come from the people, all of us. We should not be so keen to eat meat with every meal. This will affect the demand for meat, and then hopefully the practice of deforestation will slow down.

中譯 · 說明

第一個解決方法必須來自政府。受此問題衝擊的各國政府必須趕緊立法，以阻止公司掠奪土地。它們不但必須立法，還必須強力執法。這會對潛在的企業發出的訊息是，應該要守法。第二個解決方法必須來自民眾，就是我們大家。我們不該這麼貪圖每一餐都要吃肉。這將會去影響對肉品的需求，然後砍伐森林的行徑便有望減緩。

☆ 請注意我在本段又用了 A 和 B 句。A 會是我的第一個解決方法，而 B 是我的第二個方法。

☆ A 和 B 是最一般性的，接著 A1、A2 和 B1 是比較具體的結果。

☆ 希望你也是這樣標號。如果 A 和 B 的順序不一樣，請不用擔心，但希望你有看出它們是最一般性的句子。

☆ 希望你在段落中已經找到所有字彙。如果沒有，請回頭繼續找！

我們來看一些英文寫作的真題範例。

## 📝 Extra Practice Essays

請利用前面學過的重點，練習規劃以下「問題／解決方法」類型的作文題目。

**TOPIC 1** 109 年學士後中醫（慈濟）

More and more studies have shown that dementia occurs not only among seniors, but also people under the age of 60. Please write an essay around 200- 250 words to discuss the possible problems dementia patients and their families might face. Also, as a Chinese medicine doctor, how would you help your patients and their families to cope with the illness.

**TOPIC 2** 107 年學士後西醫（高醫）

**IV. Essay Writing: 20 points**

According to Social Enterprise Insights, many countries in the world are currently facing the problem of an aging population. In the case of Taiwan, its aging index is 92%. From this evidence, Taiwan's rate of aging is like an unstoppable train, with the speed surpassing that of any developed country. What are the likely impacts of an aging society on our medical system? What are the roles of medical personnel in the face of this trend? Please write a well-organized essay with at least 200 words to express your opinions.

　　在結束這個單元之前，請將下列的清單看過，確定能將所有要點都勾選起來。如果有些要點你還搞不清楚，請回頭再次研讀本單元的相關部分。

☐ 我學到了如何針對「問題／解決方法」文章來腦力激盪出想法。

☐ 我學到如何在腦力激盪中組織想法，並練習了組織我的想法。

☐ 我看到了一些「問題／解決方法」的真題範例，並練習針對它來規劃文章。

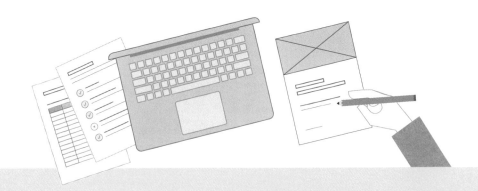

# Unit 4

## 如何規劃回答：
## 論證／意見的文章
### How to Plan Your Answer: Argument/Opinion Essay

在前一個單元你已學到要如何腦力激盪出想法，並規劃「問題／解決方法」的文章。在本單元我們則要學習如何規劃「論證／意見」的文章。

首先再來複習一下前面學過的腦力激盪。

**請針對這個題目進行腦力激盪，並把你的想法整理在下方的表格中。**

> *The mass media, including Television, radio and newspapers, have a great influence in shaping people's ideas.*
>
> *To what extent to do you agree or disagree with this statement?*

| Opinion: Agree | |
|---|---|
| **reasons I agree with this statement** | **reasons I disagree with this statement** |
| | |

解答・説明

請參考表格內容，並且閱讀下方的說明。

| Opinion: Agree | |
|---|---|
| **reasons I agree with this statement** | **reasons I disagree with this statement** |
| • positive or negative influence<br>• happens whether they want it or not<br>• TV, radio, newspaper – traditional media<br>• new media: facebook, social networking, go online, twitter, LINE<br>• exposed to ideas from<br>• virtually impossible - escape | • views shaped by other people's views<br>• come into contact with other people<br>• independent thinking<br>• influence is exaggerated |

☆ 在表格中可以看到我先決定好自己的意見是什麼，然後再把想法大致上組織成兩種類型：我贊成的原因，以及我反對的原因。

☆ 你可以看到我贊成題目的想法，所以贊成那一欄的內容比較多，但是請注意我也在反對那一欄放了一些內容。你必須稍微平衡兩方意見。

☆ 你可以看到我沒有寫完整的句子，並且主要是寫出搭配字或是片語。

☆ 此外，請注意我舉出一些具體的例子。新媒體：facebook, social networking, go online, twitter, LINE；以及傳統媒體：TV, radio, newspapers.

☆ 現在，先不要擔心我如何組織這些字。當它們出現在我腦海時，我只是把它們寫下來，然後直接放進正確的欄位。

　　你已經學過要如何在腦力激盪中產生想法，現在則需要依照在 Unit 1 所學到的 general/specific 模式來把它們組織起來。

　　如同你在前一個單元中做過的，首先要決定哪些字彙是概括性的，把那些字彙變成你的主題句。然後決定要以哪些字彙來為主題句增添特定的資訊。在組織字彙時，要想到文章的最終形式，也就是你認為會需要多少個段落。

　　我用上方 Task 1 的題目來舉例。題目再次如下。

---

*The mass media, including Television, radio and newspapers, have a great influence in shaping people's ideas.*
*To what extent to do you agree or disagree with this statement?*

---

### ✎ Task 2

請研究表格中的 **agree** 欄位，並且閱讀下方的說明。

| Opinion: Agree | |
|---|---|
| reasons I agree with this statement | reasons I disagree with this statement |
| **A3** positive or negative influence<br><br>**B1** happens whether they want it or not | • views shaped by other people's views<br><br>• come into contact with other people |

| A1 ii TV, radio, newspaper – i traditional media<br><br>B new media: facebook, social networking, go online, twitter, LINE<br><br>A2 exposed to ideas from<br><br>A virtually impossible – escape | • independent thinking<br><br>• influence is exaggerated |
| --- | --- |

☆ 注意 A 和 B，以及 A1、A2 等等的標號。

☆ A 句和 B 句是主題句。我決定要寫三個段落當作這篇文章的主體，其中兩個段落是支持論述 A 和 B，另一個段落則是批評它。

☆ 句子 A1、A2 和 A3 針對 A 句提出了具體資訊，而 B 句也是一樣的狀況。

☆ 請注意，我還有 A1i 和 A1ii：我這樣做是因為我想要讓 A1i 先出現，因為它較為概括。A1ii 則是 A1i 的具體例子。

　　來看看當我寫作時，這樣的規劃如何運作。

## ✏ Task 3

閱讀以下文章的段落並與 Task 2 中的規劃做比對，若字彙是出自 Task 2 表格裡 agree 欄位的就把它畫上底線。

> It's virtually impossible in our day to escape any kind of contact with mass media. First, anyone who uses traditional media, for example watches TV, listens to the radio or reads the newspaper is going to be exposed to ideas, and those ideas are going to influence them either positively or negatively.
>
> Secondly, even if you never watch TV or read a newspaper, anyone who goes online, logs into Facebook, or uses other social media such as twitter or LINE is also going to have their views shaped by those media, whether they want to be influenced or not.

中譯・說明

在我們這個時代，要逃避與大眾媒體的任何形式接觸簡直是不可能。首先，任何人一使用傳統媒體，例如看電視、聽收音機或看報紙，都會接觸到某些觀點，而這些想法則會帶來正面或負面的影響。

其次，就算你從不看電視或看報紙，任何人一上網、登入臉書或使用其他的社群媒體，諸如推特或 LINE，看法也會受到這些媒體所形塑，無論自己是不是想要受到影響。

☆ 希望你有找到所有的字彙，並且看出我在 Task 2 規劃的結構，如何呈現在最後的段落文章中。

好的，現在換你來試試看。

## ✏ Task 4

**請組織 Task 2 表格 disagree 欄位裡的字彙。**

參考答案

請看我如何組織 disagree 欄位的字彙，並且將它和下面的段落比較。和之前一樣，請將段落裡的字彙畫上底線。

| Opinion: Agree | |
|---|---|
| **reasons I agree with this statement** | **reasons I disagree with this statement** |
| **A3** positive or negative influence | **C2** views shaped by other people's views |
| **B1** happens whether they want it or not | **C3** come into contact with other people |
| **A1 ii** TV, radio, newspaper–**i** traditional media | **C1** independent thinking |
| **B** new media: facebook, social networking, go online, twitter, LINE | **C** influence is exaggerated |
| **A2** exposed to ideas from | |
| **A** virtually impossible–escape | |

On the other hand, there are those who argue that this influence is exaggerated, and that our thinking is independent, or influenced more by the views of other people we come into contact with. I don't agree with this, because the views of the people we meet are just as likely to be formed by mass media as well.

中譯・說明

另一方面，有人則認為這樣的影響受到了誇大，而且我們的思考具獨立性，或者較具影響力的看法更多是來自所接觸的其他人。我對此並不贊同，因為熟識之人的看法同樣很可能也是由大眾媒體所形成。

☆ 請注意我標出了 C 句，那是我的第三段。

☆ C 句是最概括性的，接著是針對 C 提出更具體細節的 C1、C2 和 C3 句。

☆ 希望你也是這樣標號。如果 C1、C2 和 C3 的順序不一樣，請不用擔心，但我希望你有看出 influence is exaggerated 是最概括性的句子，因此它應該是主題句 C。

☆ 希望你在段落中有找到所有字彙。如果沒有，請回頭繼續找！

我們來看一些英文寫作的眞題範例。

## 📝 Extra Practice Essays

請利用前面學過的重點，練習規劃以下「論證／意見」類型的作文題目。

**TOPIC 1** 106 年學士後中醫（義守）

二、作文題（共 **20** 分）

There has been a recent controversy in Taiwan over the necessity of the so-called English graduation threshold, a policy that requires enrolled students to pass certain English proficiency tests in order to graduate. One main criticism, among others, of the policy is that courses have not been offered aiming to prepare students to take the standardized tests required by the policy. The criticism, however, appears to risk a negative side of the washback effect, i.e., what to teach is influenced by what is to be tested. Please write a well-organized essay of around 200-250 words expressing your point of view and your arguments concerning the policy.

**TOPIC 2** 105 年學士後西醫（高醫）

**IV. Essay Writing: 20 points**
Please write a well-organized essay with at least 200 words to express your opinions on Human Dignity and Medical Rights.

在你結束這個單元之前，請將下列的清單看過，確定你能將所有要點都勾選起來。如果有一些要點你還搞不清楚，請回頭再次研讀本單元的相關部分。

☐ 我學到了如何針對「論證／意見」文章來腦力激盪出想法。

☐ 我學到如何在腦力激盪中組織想法，並練習了組織我的想法。

☐ 我看到了一些「論證／意見」的真題範例，並練習針對它來規劃文章。

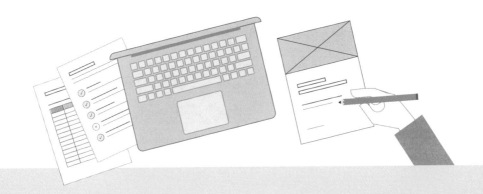

# Unit 5

## 如何寫引言：
## 論證／意見的文章
### How to Write the Introduction:
### Argument/Opinion Essay

在本單元和下一個單元裡，你會學到要如何寫文章的「引言」。我們會把重點放在引言的內容和組織，並且會看一些能運用於引言的詞語。

首先來看看範例。

**先閱讀題目和引言範例，再看下方的說明。**

題目

---

*Plans to give prisoners computers with access to the internet so that they can study while they are in prison have been criticized for wasting government money.*

*Write an essay expressing your point of view.*

---

引言

---

There is no doubt that giving inmates computers with internet access will help many convicted criminals to educate themselves for a better life after they leave prison. On the other hand, this will also cost a lot of public money, money which could be used for other things. It's my opinion that the benefits of this plan far outweigh the costs. There are many reasons why I think so.

---

中譯・說明

**【題目】**

計畫為受刑人配置上網用的電腦，好讓他們在服刑時能進修，遭到了批評是在浪費政府經費。

寫一篇文章來表達你的觀點。

**【引言】**

無庸置疑的是，為獄友配置上網用的電腦會有助於很多遭定罪的犯人自我教育，好讓他們出獄後能過上更好的生活。另一方面，這也會花費大量的公帑，而這些經費大可用在其他的事物上。依我之見，這種計畫的好處遠勝於花費。我會這麼

想的理由有很多。

........................................................................................

☆ 引言是以描述背景的句子來開頭。background「背景句」重複使用題目裡的
　字彙，但卻不是整個題目照抄。

☆ 此外，引言有 balancing「平衡句」，也就是提出另一個與題目和背景句相反的
　可能看法。這篇文章是 argument/opinion 類型，所以你必須在引言中寫論證。

☆ 引言的背景句和平衡句都很概括。它們是在表達概括性的看法，不會談論具體
　細節，或是提出特定例子。

☆ 引言有清楚的 opinion「意見句」。

☆ 引言中還包含 signposting「路標句」，說明了文章其餘的篇幅會更詳細討論意
　見。這種句子的功能在於描述文章其餘篇幅的組織。

☆ 引言相當簡短，不會超過四個句子。


　　我們現在要接著來看，引言的 background 和 balance 句該怎麼寫。


## ✏ Task 2

**請將以下 set-phrases 歸類至下方表格中。**

---

- Although this may be true in some cases, v.p.

- However, there are two sides to this statement.

- In recent years v.p.

- It cannot be denied that v.p.

- It is true to say that v.p.

- Many people believe that v.p.

- However, this is surely not the only way to look at the question.

- Many people consider that v.p.

- There is no doubt that v.p.

- However, while this may be true to some extent, v.p.

- On the other hand, v.p.

---

| background | balancing |
|---|---|
| | |

請參考表格內容，並且閱讀下方的說明。

| background | balancing |
|---|---|
| • In recent years v.p.<br>　近年來，v.p. | • Although this may be true in some cases, v.p.<br>　雖然這在某些情況下或許為真，v.p. |
| • It cannot be denied that v.p.<br>　不容否認的是，v.p. | • However, there are two sides to this statement.<br>　不過，這樣的說法有兩個方面。 |
| • It is true to say that v.p.<br>　這話說得沒錯，v.p. | • However, this is surely not the only way to look<br>　at the question.<br>　不過，這肯定不是看待問題的唯一方式。 |
| • Many people believe that v.p.<br>　很多人相信，v.p. | |
| • Many people consider that v.p.<br>　很多人認為，v.p. | • However, while this may be true to some<br>　extent, v.p.<br>　不過，這在某種程度上或許為真，v.p. |
| • There is no doubt that v.p.<br>　無庸置疑的是，v.p. | • On the other hand, v.p.<br>　另一方面，v.p. |

☆ 你可以在 problem/solution 的文章中使用背景句。但是不該在這類文章中使用平衡句。

☆ 注意，這些 set-phrases 大部分是以 v.p. 結尾，所以請確定在描述背景時，你使用的是 v.p.。

☆ 請留意 in recent years。在 v.p. 中必須使用現在完成式，例如：In recent

years, there has been a drop in the birth rate in my country. ，不可使用現在簡
單式或過去簡單式。

☆ 如果你要用 become 這個動詞，不可用在現在簡單式，要用在現在完成式。

☆ 就其他 set-phrases 來說，你應該在接下來的 v.p. 用現在簡單式。

☆ 當你在寫 balancing 的句子時，請確保你的想法的確和第一個句子形成對比。

☆ 在學這些 set-phrases 時，請確定你已完全正確地理解它們的用法。須注意小
細節，尤其是標點符號，例如，請注意哪些有逗號，以及這些逗號在哪裡。

---

❌ 錯誤

❖ In recent years, globalization <u>is</u> a big issue.

❖ In recent years, <u>there was</u> a lot of talk about democracy.

❖ In recent years, plastic waste in the sea <u>becomes</u> a big problem.

❖ On the other <u>hand it</u> is not always the case.

---

✔ 正確

❖ In recent years, globalization <u>has become</u> a big issue.

❖ In recent years, <u>there has been</u> a lot of talk about democracy.

❖ In recent years, plastic waste in the sea <u>has become</u> a big problem.

❖ On the other <u>hand, it</u> is not always the case.

---

在 Task 1 的引言中，你可以看到兩組 set-phrases：There is no doubt
that … 和 On the other hand。接下來，我們把焦點放在 set-phrases 的細節，
協助你確認自己是否已正確地理解它們的用法。

## ✏ Task 3

請把這些句子裡的錯誤加以改正。

---

**EX.** Many people believed that prison is only for punishment and not for
deterrent.

*Many people believe that prison is only for punishment and not for deterrent.*

---

1. There is not doubt that giving prisoners opportunities to study in prison is a good idea

   → _____

2. It cannot be denied giving prisoners computers with internet access.

   → _____

3. It is true saying that the plan will cost a lot of public money.

   → _____

4. In recent years the number of prisoners increases.

   → _____

5. Many people consider that giving prisoners computers with internet access.

   → _____

6. However, while this may be true to extent, there are other ways of considering the question.

   → _____

7. Although this may be true in some case, some prisoners might become rehabilitated if they can study in prison

   → _____

解答・中譯・說明

EX. Many people believe that prison is only for punishment and not for deterrent.
很多人相信，監禁只是為了懲罰，而不是為了嚇阻。

1. There is **no** doubt that giving prisoners opportunities to study in prison is a good idea.
無庸置疑的是，讓受刑人有機會在服刑時進修是個好主意。

2. It cannot be denied **that** giving prisoners computers with internet access **is controversial**.

不容否認的是，為受刑人配置上網用的電腦是有爭議的。

3. It is true **to say** that the plan will cost a lot of public money.

的確，這項計畫將會花費大量的公帑。

4. In recent years the number of prisoners **has been increasing**.

近年來，受刑人的數目有增無減。

5. Many people consider that giving prisoners computers with internet access **is a waste of money**.

很多人認為，為受刑人配置上網用的電腦是浪費錢。

6. However, while this may be true to **some** extent, there are other ways of considering the question.

不過，雖然這在某種程度上或許為真，但這個問題有很多別的考量方式。

7. Although this may be true in some **cases**, some prisoners might become rehabilitated if they can study in prison.

雖然這在某些情況下或許為真，但假如能在服刑時進修，有些受刑人或許會改過自新。

················································································

☆ 請注意 2. 和 5. 都是錯在 n.p. 和 v.p.，其他則遺漏一些東西，或是稍微改變一些字。

☆ 4. 的 set-phrase 後面的 v.p. 動詞時態有錯誤。

☆ 請注意哪些句子少了標點符號。

☆ 請務必確認自己已正確地學習並使用這些 set-phrases，特別是小細節。

## 🖉 Task 4

練習運用到目前為止所學過的重點，將句子依適當的順序排列以形成下方作文題目的引言。

> *Governments should legislate to ensure that women have the same opportunities as men in the market for labour.*
> *Write an essay expressing your point of view.*

A  I do not believe that it's the job of government to pass laws to make sure companies recruit equal numbers of men and women.

B On the other hand, some companies might find it difficult to recruit men and women in equal numbers, due to the nature of the labour market, or due to the kind of work being offered.

C There are two main reasons why I think so.

D There is no doubt that women should have the same chances to find jobs as men.

1. _____ 2._____ 3._____ 4. _____

解答・中譯・說明

【題目】

政府應該要立法來確保女性在勞動市場上跟男性具有相同的機會。

撰寫一篇文章來表達你的觀點。

【引言】（依適當順序）

D 無庸置疑的是，女性應該要有與男性相同的求職機會。

B 另一方面，基於勞動市場的性質或基於所開出職務的種類，有些公司或許會發現難以聘用相同人數的男女。

A 我相信通過法令來確保公司聘用相同人數的男女並非政府的工作。

C 我為什麼會這麼想，主要的理由有二。

☆ 針對這個題目，引言的適當順序應該是 D、B、A、C。其中 D 和 B 是背景句和平衡句，A 是意見句，C 則是路標句。

✏ Task 5

請閱讀下面的 argument/opinion 寫作題目，然後用你在本單元學到的方法和用語寫一段引言。

> *Some people believe that children are naturally competitive, and that this should be encouraged in order to prepare them for the adult world. Others think that children should be taught to cooperate instead.*
> *Discuss both these views and give your own opinion.*

**【題目】**

有的人相信，兒童是天生就會競爭，而且對此應該要加以鼓勵，好讓他們為成人世界做好準備。有的人則認為，應該要教兒童合作才對。

對這些看法都加以討論，並提出自身的意見。

**【範例答案】**

There is no doubt that children like to compete against each other, and that they like to win. However, while this may be true to some extent, in the real world, cooperation is just as important. It's my opinion that children need to learn how to compete fairly and how to cooperate usefully, in order to prepare them for the world they will face as adults. There are three main reasons why.

毫無疑問，孩子們喜歡互相競爭，他們喜歡獲勝。然而，儘管這在某種程度上可能是正確的，但在現實世界中，合作同樣重要。依我之見，孩子們需要學習如何公平競爭以及如何有效合作，以便為他們成年後將要面對的世界做好準備。主要有以下三個理由。

☆ 我當然不知道你寫了什麼，但希望你寫了一些和參考答案相仿的內容。

☆ 請注意句子的順序是 background、balance、opinion、signposting。

☆ 請注意題目中的字彙如何被替換使用。

☆ 請注意意見中表達同意兩者看法的方式。

## ✐ Task 6

請仔細閱讀第 64, 97, 121, 145 頁的 **Reading** 範例文章，並找出各篇文章之引言所使用的 **set-phrases**。

在 Reading 1 中，你會看到 Many people believe that 和 However, while this may be true to some extent。在 Reading 2 中，希望你看到了 There is no doubt that。在 Reading 3 中，你應該找到了 It cannot be denied that。在 Reading 4 中，則是有 On the other hand。

我們來看一些英文寫作的真題範例。

## 📝 Extra Practice Essays

請利用前面學過的重點，練習針對以下題目來撰寫「引言」。

**TOPIC 1** 110 年學士後西醫（高醫）

> **IV. Essay Writing: 20 points.**
> **Write an essay of at least 200 words in an appropriate style on the following topic.**
> The Ministry of Health and Welfare has set a goal to vaccinate 60% of the population with a COVID-19 vaccine. Do you agree or disagree with the goal set by the Ministry? Use specific reasons to support your answer(s).

**TOPIC 2** 111 年學士後西醫（中興）

> **IV. Essay Writing: 20 points.**
> It is generally known that the job of a physician is highly stressful. If you are admitted to a medical college, what do you propose to do to prepare yourself for the extraordinary pressures and challenges that lie ahead? Write a well-organised essay of at least 200 words to elaborate on your ideas.

在你結束這個單元之前，請將下列的清單看過，確定你能將所有要點都勾選起來。如果有一些要點你還搞不清楚，請回頭再次研讀本單元的相關部分。

☐ 我學到了如何寫「論證／意見」類型文章的引言。

☐ 我學會使用一些 set-phrases 來表達背景和平衡。

☐ 我學到了在使用 set-phrases 時，所應避免的一些常見錯誤。

☐ 我練習去寫了「論證／意見」文章的引言。

☐ 我看到了一些真題範例，並針對那些題目練習寫了引言。

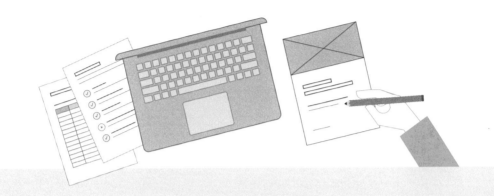

# Unit 6

## 如何寫引言：
## 問題／解決方法的文章

### How to Write the Introduction:
### Problem/Solution Essay

在前一個單元裡，你學到了要如何在「論證／意見」
文章的引言中帶入背景和平衡句。在本單元我們則
會學到要如何表達意見，以及如何把文章其餘部分
的組織帶出來。

本單元的詞語於「論證／意見」和「問題／解決方法」類型的文章皆可使用。首先來看一個範例：

✏ **Task 1**

**請閱讀文章題目、引言範例，以及下方的說明。**

題目

> *Rising sea levels caused by global warming is one of the biggest problems humanity faces, both now and in the future.*
> *What other problems are associated with this, and what are some possible solutions?*

引言

> In recent years, rising sea levels have threatened many low-lying parts of the world. This has caused serious flooding and other problems for some of the world's major cities and industrial zones. It's my opinion that national governments alone can not solve this problem, and that it needs an international response. I can think of two solutions to this problem, one long term, and one short term.

中譯・說明

**【題目】**
全球暖化造成海平面上升是人類所面臨的最大問題之一，現在和未來皆然。
還有哪些其他問題與此相關，有哪些可能的解決方法？

**【引言】**
近年來，海平面上升威脅到了世界上很多的低窪地區。這對世界上一些大型的城市與工業區造成了嚴重的水患和其他問題。依我之見，光靠各國政府並不能解決這個問題，它需要的是國際社會的回應。對於這個問題，我想到兩種解決的方

法，一種是長期的，一種是短期的。

☆ 請注意句子的順序是 background、opinion、signposting。你不應該在這種文章使用 balancing 句，因為題目並未要你提出論證，也沒有要你探討問題的正反面。題目只是要你描述一個問題，並提出解決方法。

☆ 請注意前面學到的 set-phrases 用法。

☆ 請注意 can 和 need 這兩個助動詞的用法。你將必須在 problem/solution 的文章使用這樣的助動詞，而且會在稍後學到更多使用它們的方法。

☆ 文章其餘的篇幅，可能會先用一個簡短的段落提出例子，討論其他因海平面上升所引發的問題，然後再寫兩個段落來描述一些長期的解決方法，最後是一個簡短的結語。

　　現在，我們來看你可以使用哪些用語表達自己的意見，以及作爲 signposting 在引言中提出你文章的概要。

## ✏ Task 2

**請將以下 set-phrases 分類放進表格中。**

> - I disagree with the view that v.p.
> - There are many reasons why I think so.
> - I do not believe that v.p.
> - It's my opinion that v.p.
> - There are many ways to solve this problem.
> - I (dis)agree with this, and think that v.p.
> - This essay will look at some of the common problems and will then suggest two solutions.
> - I can think of two solutions to this problem.
> - There are two/three main reasons.
> - I firmly believe that v.p.
> - There's no doubt in my mind that v.p.

| opinion set-phrases | signposting set-phrases |
|---|---|
| | |

請參考表格內容，並且閱讀下方的說明。

| opinion set-phrases | signposting set-phrases |
|---|---|
| • I firmly believe that v.p.<br>　我堅信 v.p.<br><br>• It's my opinion that v.p.<br>　依我之見 v.p.<br><br>• I (dis)agree with the view that v.p.<br>　我（不）贊同的看法是 v.p.<br><br>• There's no doubt in my mind that v.p.<br>　在我的心目中，無庸置疑的是 v.p.<br><br>• I do not believe that v.p.<br>　我不相信 v.p.<br><br>• I (dis)agree with this, and think that v.p.<br>　我（不）贊同這點，並認為 v.p. | • There are many reasons why I think so.<br>　我為什麼會這麼想，理由有很多。<br><br>• There are two/three main reasons.<br>　主要的理由有二／三。<br><br>• I can think of two solutions to this problem.<br>　對於這個問題，我能想到兩個解決方法。<br><br>• This essay will look at some of the common problems and will then suggest two solutions.<br>　本短文會來看一些常見的問題，然後建議兩個解決方法。<br><br>• There are many ways to solve this problem.<br>　這個問題的解決方式有很多。 |

☆ 你當然可以用 In my opinion 來表達意見，但這樣寫並不高明，無法讓你得到高分。請嘗試用一些其他的 set-phrases。

☆ This essay will argue that v.p. 是非常學術和客觀的陳述方式。你可以在 problem/solution 的文章使用以下三個 set-phrases：I can think of two solutions to this problem. / There are many ways to solve this problem. / This essay will look at some of the common problems and will then suggest two solutions.。在稍後將會看到更多範例。

☆ 請記得，當你學習和使用這些 set-phrases，要確定自己完全正確地了解所有小細節，尤其是字尾和小詞。

---

❌ 錯誤

❖ I <u>disagree the view</u> that governments should legislate on gender equality.

❖ I <u>firm</u> believe that governments should legislate on gender equality.

❖ There are many <u>reason</u> why I think so.

❖ There are many <u>way</u> to solve this problem.

---

✅ 正確

❖ I disagree <u>with</u> the view that governments should legislate on gender equality.

❖ I <u>firmly</u> believe that governments should legislate on gender equality.

❖ There are many <u>reasons</u> why I think so.

❖ There are many <u>ways</u> to solve this problem.

---

在 Task 1 的引言中，你可以看到兩組 set-phrases：It's my opinion that 和 I can think of two solutions to this problem。接下來，我們把焦點放在 set-phrases 的細節，協助你確認自己是否已正確地理解它們的用法。

### 📝 Task 3

請看下列句子，找出 **set-phrases** 裡的錯誤並且修正它們。我們來看看範例。

**EX.** I firmly believed that we need to give this problem our most urgent attention.

*I firmly believe that we need to give this problem our most urgent attention.*

1. There's no doubt that this is a serious problem.

   →  _____

2. There's not a doubt in my mind that together we can solve this issue.

   →  _____

3. I agree this and think it should be possible.

   →  _____

4. There are many reason why I think so.

   →  _____

5. I can think of two solution to this problem.

   →  _____

6. There are many way to solve this problems.

   →  _____

7. This essay will look at some of the common problem and will then suggest two solution.

   →  _____

解答・中譯・說明

EX. *I firmly believe that* we need to give this problem our most urgent attention.
   我堅信我們需要對此問題投以最迫切的關注。

1. There's no doubt **in my mind** that this is a serious problem.
   在我看來，這無疑是個嚴重的問題。

2. There's no ~~a~~ doubt in my mind that together we can solve this issue.
   在我心中無庸置疑的是，我們能一起來解決這個課題。

3. I agree **with** this and think it should be possible.
   我贊同這點，並認為這應該是有可能的。

4. There are many reason**s** why I think so.

　　我為什麼會這麼想，理由有很多。

5. I can think of two solution**s** to this problem.

　　對於這個問題，我能想到兩個解決方法。

6. There are many way**s** to solve this problem.

　　這個問題的解決方式有很多。

7. This essay will look at some of the common problem**s** and will then suggest two solution**s**.

　　本文會來看一些常見的問題，然後建議兩個解決方案。

----

☆ 請注意 There's no doubt in my mind 和 There's no doubt that … 的差別。前者是表達意見的 set-phrase，後者則是我們在上個單元所學到的描述背景的 set-phrase。

☆ 留意到第三題漏了小詞：with。

☆ 其餘的 set-phrase 全都在關鍵單字上少了 s。對於單字的結尾，需要非常小心。

☆ 務必要學會並準確使用這些 set-phrases。要聚焦於小細節。

## ✎ Task 4

練習運用到目前為止所學過的重點，將句子依適當的順序排列以形成下方作文題目的引言。

> *The anti-vaxxer movement – people who refused to get vaccinated against COVID - has spread across the world, putting lives at risk, and also increasing the risk that new variants such as OMICRON may appear. What are some of the reasons people refuse to get vaccinated and what can be done about this problem?*

A I firmly believe that citizens and city governments have the responsibility to look for solutions to this problem.

B It cannot be denied that the anti-vaxxer movement is one of the most serious issues facing the fight against disease.

C This essay will suggest two solutions.

D Vaccines are generally safe and there is no good reason why people should not get vaccinated.

1. _____ 2. _____ 3. _____ 4. _____

解答‧中譯‧說明

【題目】

拒絕接種 COVID 疫苗的人把反疫苗分子的運動散布到了全世界，置生命於險境，並增加了諸如 OMICRON 等新變種出現的風險。人們拒絕接種疫苗的一些理由是什麼，而針對這個問題可以做些什麼？

【引言】（依適當順序）

B 不容否認的是，反疫苗分子的運動是對抗疾病所面臨的最嚴重課題之一。

D 疫苗通常是很安全的，人們並沒有充分的理由不去接種疫苗。

A 我堅信，國民和政府有責任為這個問題尋求解決之道。

C 本文會建議兩個解決方式。

☆ 針對這個題目，引言的適當順序應該是：B、D、A、C。其中 B 是背景句，D 是在為短文後段所要闡揚的背景句來勾勒更多的資訊。A 是意見句，C 則是路標句。由於這是「問題／解決方法」類型文章，所以沒有平衡句。

### ✎ Task 5

**請閱讀下面的 problem/solution 寫作題目，然後用你在本單元學到的方法和用語寫一段引言。**

> *Overpopulation of urban areas is causing many problems for citizens. What are some of the most serious ones, and what can individuals and governments do to solve these problems?*

解答‧中譯‧說明

【題目中譯】

都市地區人口過剩對市民造成許多問題。

其中哪些是最嚴重的問題，而個人和政府能做什麼來解決這些問題？

【範例答案】

It cannot be denied that one of the most serious problems inhabitants of big cities face is the problem of overcrowding. Too many people are crowding together in spaces that were not designed or built for so many people. I firmly believe that citizens and city governments have the responsibility to look for solutions to this problem. This essay will suggest two solutions.

不容否認的是，大城市的居民所面臨最嚴重的問題之一就是過度擁擠。太多人一起擠在並非為這麼多人所設計或建造的空間裡。我堅信，市民和市政府有責任為這個問題尋求解決之道。本文會建議兩個解決方案。

☆ 我當然不知道你寫了什麼，但希望你寫了一些和參考答案相仿的內容。

☆ 請注意句子的順序是 background、opinion、signposting。

☆ 請注意所用到的 set-phrases。

☆ 文章的其餘部分可能會先討論人口過剩所造成的其他一些問題，並以一小段來舉例，然後用一段來描述個人層次的解決方法，再以一段來描述一些政府層次的解決方法。

## ✎ Task 6

請仔細閱讀第 64, 97, 121, 145 頁的 **Reading** 範例文章，並找出各篇文章之引言所使用的 **set-phrases**。

解答・說明

• 在 Reading 1 中有 I firmly believe that 和 There are two main reasons why I think so。

• 在 Reading 2 中應該是有 This essay will look at some of the common problems caused by overpopulation and will then suggest two solutions。

• 在 Reading 3 中是有 It's my opinion that 和 This essay will look at some of the common problems and will then suggest two solutions。

• 在 Reading 4 中，希望你找到了 I agree that 和 There are many reasons why I think so。

為了總結我們在寫作引言上所下的工夫，以下是你可以參考學習的重點清單。

---

**Writing an introduction checklist**

1. 重複使用題目的字彙，但不要照抄。
2. 從 background「背景句」開始寫。
3. 只有在「論證／意見」文章中才使用 balancing「平衡句」來寫你的論證。
4. 請寫一個 opinion「意見句」。
5. 用 signposting「路標句」當作結尾。
6. 請表達概括性的內容，不要提出具體的例子或細節。

---

我們來看一些英文寫作的真題範例。

### 📝 Extra Practice Essays

**請利用前面學過的重點，練習針對以下題目來撰寫「引言」。**

**TOPIC 1** 110 年學士後中醫（義守）

In your opinion, can any subject of humanities (such as literature, history, art, music, or sociology) be useful in medical education and clinical practice? Please give your answer and explain why (in at least 250 words). You may focus on one or more subjects or give one or more examples in your discussion.

**IV. Essay Writing: 20 points.**

**Write an essay of at least 200 words in an appropriate style on the following topic.**

As a medical practitioner, you may need to face patients and families with strong emotions, especially when the patient's conditions are critical. In what ways do you think it is important to deal with the emotions of the patients and families, and what will be your strategies to deal with them. Use examples to elaborate on your response.

在你結束這個單元之前，請將下列的清單看過，確定你能將所有要點都勾選起來。如果有一些要點你還搞不清楚，請回頭再次研讀本單元的相關部分。

□ 我學到了如何寫「問題／解決方法」類型文章的引言。

□ 我學會使用一些 set-phrases 來表達意見和路標句。

□ 我學到了在使用 set-phrases 時，所應避免的一些常見錯誤。

□ 我練習去寫了「問題／解決方法」文章的引言。

□ 我看到了一些真題範例，並針對那些題目練習寫了引言。

# Reading 1
## sample essay: argument/opinion

閱讀以下寫作題目及範例文章。請留意兩個正文段落之主題句,你能不能看出這兩句是如何最為概括,以及段落中的其他各句是如何發展或對主題句提供具體的細節?

寫作題目

> The government should not support the arts. The money will be better spent on other things.
> To what extent do you agree or disagree?

範例文章

Many people believe that art is something which only a few people are interested in, and that because of this the government should not spend public money on it. However, while this may be true to some extent, nonetheless, the arts play a significant role in public life. I firmly believe that the government should support the arts. There are two main reasons why I think so.

First, the arts provide employment to lots of people who have highly specialised skills. Actors, dancers, musicians and theatre and film technicians, for example, often have highly developed skills which take years of training to develop. However, without state support, the institutions where such people train will not survive, and the people who work in those institutions will also be out of work. Also, opera houses and theatres which receive state funding employ many people, not only in the big cities, but also when they tour outside the cities.

Second, some people think that the government should only spend money on things which benefit the whole of society, such as education, health and defence. Although the benefits of spending on the arts may be difficult to measure, that doesn't mean that there are no tangible benefits for the nation as a whole. Take my country (UK) for example. The theatre industry in London is world famous and millions of tourists go to see a musical or visit museums when they come to London. This kind of tourist attraction brings in revenue for the state. Without initial government funding, many of the sights the tourists come to see would never have been created.

To summarize, it is my opinion that the arts are important for everyone, and the benefits of the state supporting them far outweigh the costs.

中譯

政府不該金援藝術。經費投注在別的事物上會更好。
你是在什麼程度上贊同或不贊同？

很多人相信，藝術是只有少數人才感興趣的東西，所以政府不該投注公共經費在此。然而，儘管這在某種程度上或許為真，但藝術在公共生活上發揮了重要作用。我堅信，政府應該要金援藝術。我為什麼會這麼想，主要的理由有二。

一，藝術為許多具備高度專門技能的人提供了就業。例如演員、舞者、樂手和影劇技術人員常具備了高度發展的技能，要花費多年的訓練才能養成。不過在少了公家的金援下，訓練這類人員的機構就會無法存續，在這些機構裡工作的人也會失業。另外，獲得公家資助的歌劇院和劇場會雇用很多人，不僅是在大城市裡，在城市以外的地方巡迴時也是如此。

二，有些人認為，政府只該把經費投注在對社會整體有好處的事物上，諸如教育、衛生和國防。雖然投注在藝術上的好處或許難以衡量，但這並不意謂著對整個國家沒有實質的好處。以我國（英國）為例，倫敦的劇場業是舉世聞名，成千上百萬的觀光客在到訪倫敦時會去看歌舞劇或是逛博物館。這種觀光賣點便會為公家帶來營收。少了最初的政府資助，觀光客到訪所看到的很多景點就絕不會被創造出來。

總之，我認為藝術對每個人都很重要，由公家金援藝術的好處遠遠超過其成本。

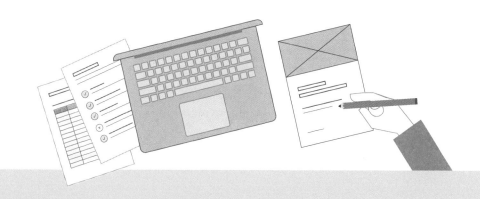

# Unit 7

## 如何為主題句添加資訊
### How to Add Information to the Topic Sentence

本單元將學習如何透過添加資訊、想法來發展主題句。

首先要特別注意的是，在添加想法時，必須確保爲主題句所增添的資訊不是特定的例子，也不是對比或不贊同的意見。

## ✎ Task 1

**根據主題句，選出可添加的資訊或想法。**

> EX. | 主題句 | Smoking is bad for your health.
> 抽菸對你的健康有害。
>
> | 加入資訊 |　　E

1. | 主題句 | Exercise is good for your physical health.
   運動對你的身體健康有益。

   | 加入資訊 | _____

2. | 主題句 | The arts teach us how to be true to ourselves.
   藝術教會我們要如何忠於自己。

   | 加入資訊 | _____

3. | 主題句 | Social media has many benefits.
   社群媒體有很多好處。

   | 加入資訊 | _____

---

A Exercise makes you feel happy.
　運動會讓你覺得快樂。

B Exercise often hurts and can cause physical problems.
　運動經常會受傷，並可能會造成身體上的問題。

C Facebook is the most popular social media site for my generation.
　臉書是我這一代最普及的社群媒體網站。

D It is also good for your mental health.
它也對你的心理健康有益。

E It is bad for the health of the people around you.
它對周遭眾人的健康有害。

F It is very popular.
它非常普及。

G Smoking causes shortness of breath and high blood pressure.
抽菸會造成呼吸急促和高血壓。

H Smoking is very enjoyable and helps to relax people.
抽菸是非常令人愉快的，而且有助於讓人放鬆。

I Social media has many dangers.
社群媒體有許多危險之處。

J The arts simply help us to pass the time and they have no usefulness.
藝術就只是有助於我們打發時間，並沒有用處可言。

K The theatre unites the individual with society because we are part of an
audience.
戲劇會把個人與社會凝聚起來，因為我們是觀眾的一部分。

L They teach us how to be good citizens.
它教我們要怎麼當個好公民。

解答・說明

1. D　2. L　3. F

☆ 請注意，正確的解答只是在為主題句增添新資訊。它並沒有舉出特定的例子，
也沒有提出相反或對比的資訊。

## ✎ Task 2

請研究表格裡的用語、例句及下方的說明。

| adding ideas | |
|---|---|
| • A further point to consider is n.p.<br>進一步要考慮到的重點在於 n.p. | • Another reason why v.p. is that v.p.<br>為什麼 v.p. 的另一個理由在於 v.p. |
| • Also,<br>另外 | • In addition to this, v.p.<br>除此之外，v.p. |
| • Another good thing about n.p. is that v.p.<br>n.p. 的另一個好處在於 v.p. | • In addition, v.p.<br>此外，v.p. |
| • Another good thing is that v.p.<br>另一個好處在於 v.p. | • Not only that, but also v.p.<br>不僅如此，而且 v.p. |
| • Another n.p. is that v.p.<br>另一樣 n.p. 是 v.p. | • … not only n.p., but also v.p. …<br>不僅是 n.p.，而且 v.p. |
| | • On top of that,<br>最重要的是 |

| sample sentences |
|---|

• Smoking has many dangers for the smoker. Another danger of smoking is that it has the same negative effects on bystanders.
抽菸對癮君子來說有許多危險之處。抽菸的另一個危險之處在於，它對旁人具同樣的負面效應。

• Social media helps families to stay in touch. In addition to this, it also helps people stay informed.
社群媒體有助於家人保持聯繫。除此之外，它還有助於民眾保持消息靈通。

• The arts are important for a civilized society. A further point to consider is the employment that the arts offer to many people.
藝術對文明社會很重要。要進一步考慮到的重點在於，藝術為很多人所提供的就業機會。

---

☆ 在台灣，人們常用 moreover 和 furthermore 來新增資訊。可惜的是，在英文裡它們很少出現，甚至很少被使用。因為這些字聽起來很不自然，所以最好盡可能避免使用它們。相對的，請盡量用上方表格中列出的字。

☆ 請注意，當你用 Another n.p. is that v.p. 的句型時，一定要重複上一個句子的名詞片語。請看上面的第一個例句。

☆ 在使用這些用語時，你必須非常小心 n.p. 和 v.p. 之間的差異。

☆ 此外，請務必小心一切的細節：小詞、字尾，確定你完整使用了 set-phrase，並且注意每一個標點符號。

☆ 請確保你要寫的想法不是具體的例子，也不是對比的意見。

接下來的練習，請聚焦於 set-phrases 的細節。

## ✏ Task 3

請將下列各句中的字詞重組成語意正確的句子。

> **EX.** A further benefits to point is exercise the of frequent consider
> *A further point to consider is the benefits of frequent exercise.*

1. Another exercise health thing that about mental good regular has is it benefits

   → _____

2. Not also that but many exercise has only benefits

   → _____

3. Another why reason is health good for you has is mental exercise that it many benefits

   → _____

4. On around of, bad smoking that is for the top people you

   → _____

EX. 還有一點需要進一步考慮的是頻繁運動的好處。

1. Another good thing about regular exercise is that it has mental health benefits.

規律運動的另一個好處在於它對心理健康有益。

2. Not only that, but also exercise has many benefits.

不僅如此,運動還有很多好處。

3. Another reason why exercise is good for you is that it has many mental health benefits.

為什麼運動對你有益的另一個理由在於,它對心理健康有好處。

4. On top of that, smoking is bad for the people around you.

最重要的是,抽菸對你周遭的人有害。

　　現在來看 set-phrases 的一些常見錯誤。

## ✏ Task 4

**請仔細研讀這些常見錯誤。**

❌ 錯誤

❖ On top of that <u>reason</u>, there is another benefit.

❖ Another good thing about the arts is that <u>social benefits</u>.

❖ Cycling is good for your physical health. <u>In addition</u>, it helps your blood circulation.

✔ 正確

❖ <u>On top of that,</u> there is another benefit.

❖ Another good thing about the arts is that <u>there are many social benefits</u>.

❖ Cycling is good for your physical health. In addition, <u>it helps to keep the environment clean</u>.

## ✎ Task 5

請仔細閱讀第 64 頁的「Reading 1 範例文章」，並找出文章中舉例說明 (illustrating) 的用語。

解答・說明

☆ 在 Reading 1 裡，你會在第一個正文落段中找到兩個添加資訊時的用語： Also, 和 … not only n.p. but also。

☆ 請注意，在 Also, 後面的句子新增了其他論點至主題句，但是並沒有舉例或與 它對比。

☆ in the big cities 和 outside the cities 是相同層次的意見，它們不是特定的例 子，也不是在對比。

## ✎ Task 6

請把這些句子裡的錯誤加以改正。

1. A further point consider is that smoking is very common, especially among men.

→ _____

2. Also many people enjoy it.

→ _____

3. Another good thing about it that it's cheap.

→ _____

4. In addition this, it's easy to do.

→ _____

5. In addition it's not easy to do.

→ _____

6. On top of that reason many people do not enjoy it.

　　→ _____

7. Not only that but many people are happy with it.

　　→ _____

8. Most people said they preferred not Facebook, but they liked Instagram.

　　→ _____

解答・中譯

1. A further point **to** consider is that smoking is very common, especially among men.
   需要進一步考慮到的點在於，抽菸非常常見，尤其是在男性之間。

2. Also**,** many people enjoy it.
   另外，很多人都樂在其中。

3. Another good thing about it **is** that it's cheap.
   它的另一個好處在於便宜。

4. In addition **to** this, it's easy to do.
   除此之外，這很容易做到。

5. In addition, it's not easy to do.
   此外，這並不容易做到。

6. On top of that**,** ~~reason~~ many people do not enjoy it.
   最重要的是，很多人並不樂在其中。

7. Not only that**,** but **also** many people are happy with it.
   不僅是這樣，而且很多人對它很滿意。

8. Most people said they preferred not **only** Facebook, but **also** they liked Instagram.
   大部分的人都說自己不僅偏好臉書，也喜歡 Instagram。

## ✎ Task 7

請回到 Task 1，用添加資訊 (adding) 的方式將句子 D、L、F 加入主題句中。來看看範例。

> **EX.** Smoking is bad for your health. *Not only that, but also it is bad for the health of the people around you.*

1. Exercise is good for your physical health.

_____

2. The arts teach us how to be true to ourselves.

_____

3. Social media has many benefits.

_____

解答‧中譯

請研讀我的範例，並確定你了解它們是怎麼寫出來的。

EX. 抽菸對你的健康有害。不僅如此，它還對你周遭眾人的健康有害。

1. Exercise is good for your physical health. *Another good thing about exercise is that it is good for your mental health.*
   運動對你的身體健康有益。運動的另一個好處在於，它也對你的心理健康有益。

2. The arts teach us how to be true to ourselves. *In addition to this, they teach us how to be good citizens.*
   藝術教會我們要如何忠於自己。除此之外，它還教我們要怎麼當個好公民。

3. Social media has many benefits. *Also, it is very popular.*
   社群媒體有很多好處。而且，它非常普及。

　　我們來看一些英文寫作的真題範例。

## 📝 Extra Practice Essays

利用前面學過的重點，練習針對以下題目來寫短文。請聚焦於為主題句添加資訊。

**TOPIC 1** 109 年學士後中醫（義守）

> What have you learned from the pandemic (COVID 19)? Please write an essay to share your personal experience of virus spread prevention in at least 250 words in English.

**TOPIC 2** 108 年學士後西醫（高醫）

> **IV. Essay Writing: 20 points**
> **Write an essay of at least 200 words in an appropriate style on the following topic.**
> In recent years, a wide range of medical robots have been in use. Inevitably, more and more work in the medical field will be done not only by us humans. Discuss how medical doctors can work with robots to help their patients in the future.

在你結束這個單元之前，請將下列的清單看過，確定你能將所有要點都勾選起來。如果有一些要點你還搞不清楚，請回頭再次研讀本單元的相關部分。

　　□ 我知道該如何為主題句添加資訊。
　　□ 我學到了一些用於表達添加資訊的 set-phrases。
　　□ 我確實知道在使用 set-phrases 時，所要避免的一些常見錯誤。
　　□ 我已經練習過如何使用這些 set-phrases。
　　□ 我看到了一些真題範例，並針對那些題目練習寫了文章。

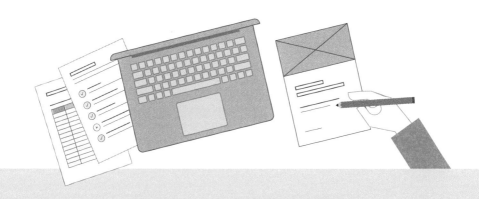

# Unit 8

## 如何舉出具體的例子
**How to Give Specific Examples**

本單元將學習如何根據前一句話的概括重點舉
出具體、特定的例子以闡述想法。

請確實完成本單元的任務。

## ✎ Task 1

根據主題句的概括說明，選出可作為具體實例的句子。

EX. 概括說明 Smoking is bad for your health. Not only that, but also it is bad for the health of the people around you.

具體實例 ___G___

1. 概括說明 Exercise is good for your physical health. Another good thing about exercise is that it is good for your mental health.

具體實例 _____

2. 概括說明 The arts teach us how to be true to ourselves. In addition to this, they teach us how to be good citizens.

具體實例 _____

3. 概括說明 Social media has many benefits. Also, it is very popular.

具體實例 _____

---

A Exercise makes you feel happy.

B Exercise often hurts and can cause physical problems.

C Facebook is the most popular social media site for my generation.

D It is also good for your mental health.

E It is bad for the health of the people around you.

F It is very popular.

G Smoking causes shortness of breath and high blood pressure.

H Smoking is very enjoyable and helps to relax people.

I Social media has many dangers.

J The arts simply help us to pass the time and they have no usefulness.

解答・說明

1. A　2. K　3. C

☆ 請注意，解答的句子是在為前一句概括說明的主題句舉出具體的例子。

## ✏ Task 2

請研究表格裡的用語、例句及下方的說明。

| illustrating ideas | |
|---|---|
| • Take for example the way that v.p.<br>就舉例來說 v.p.<br><br>• Take n.p. for example.<br>以 n.p. 為例<br><br>• For example, 例如<br><br>• For instance, 例如<br><br>• A good example here is n.p., which v.p.<br>此處很好的一個例子是 n.p.，v.p. | • A good example here is the way that v.p.<br>此處很好的一個例子就是 v.p.<br><br>• In my country, 在我國<br><br>• In my situation, 以我的處境來說<br><br>• On a personal level,<br>在個人的層次上<br><br>• …, such as… 諸如<br><br>• .., like… 像是 |
| **sample sentences** | |

• Smoking is very bad for your health. Take cancer for example, it is known that the number one cause of lung cancer is smoking.
抽菸對你的健康非常有害。以癌症為例，眾所皆知肺癌的頭號成因就是抽菸。

• The arts provide employment for many people. A good example here is the way that even a small opera house or theatre provides employment for many technicians and others.
藝術為很多人提供了就業機會。在此有個很好的例子是，連小型的歌劇院或劇院都為很多技術人員和其他人提供了就業機會。

- Social media is great for keeping people informed about events. A good example here is Facebook, which can be used in the event of an emergency to let people know you are ok.

  社群媒體非常適合讓人對事件保持消息靈通。臉書就是一個很好的例子，在事態緊急時可用它來讓別人知道你沒事。

☆ 你可以在句子中間使用 for example 和 for instance，也可以在一系列例子的前面或後面使用。但是若你這樣做，請記得不要用大寫，並確定標點符號正確。

☆ Such as 只會出現在句子中間，和 like 一樣。不要用 such like。

☆ 務必留意標點符號和 set-phrase 的其他細節，並確保你已正確使用它們。

☆ 使用 In my country、In my situation、On a personal level 時，可以舉出趣聞，或是描述某種個人經驗。在這種情況下，一定要記得用過去簡單式來描述過去的經驗。

☆ 此外，請注意你何時必須使用 n.p. 和 v.p.

接下來的練習，請聚焦於 set-phrases 的細節。

### ✎ Task 3

**請將下列各句中的字詞重組成語意正確的句子。**

> **EX.** Take impacts the around way that for others example smoking you.
> *Take for example the way that smoking impacts others around you.*

1. A Facebook example for is good around which has here been years

   → _____

2. A good introduced here is example that the Instagram way has Reels

   → _____

3. Take for Twitter example

   → _____

4. There many Instagram are networking tiktok social such sites Twitter and as

→ _____

解答・中譯

EX. 舉例來說，抽菸會衝擊到周遭的他人。

1. A good example here is Facebook which has been around for years.

一個很好的例子是已經存在多年的 Facebook。

2. A good example here is the way that Instagram has introduced Reels.

有個很好的例子就是，Instagram 引進了連續短片 (Reels)。

3. Take Twitter for example.

以推特為例。

4. There are many social networking sites such as tiktok, Twitter and Instagram.

社群網站有很多，諸如抖音、推特和 Instagram。

現在來看 set-phrases 的一些常見錯誤。

## ✏ Task 4

**請仔細研讀這些常見錯誤。**

❌ 錯誤

❖ The benefits include <u>For example</u>, low cost, high visibility, and ease of access.

❖ There are many social media platforms in my country, <u>such like</u> LINE, Whatsapp, and Facebook.

❖ Cycling has many health benefits. Take for example the way that <u>increased heart rate</u>.

✔ 正確

❖ The benefits include<u>, for example,</u> low cost, high visibility, and ease of access.

- There are many social media platforms in my country, <u>such as</u> LINE, Whatsapp, and Facebook.
- Cycling has many health benefits. Take for example the way that <u>it increases</u> your heart rate.

## ✎ Task 5

請仔細閱讀第 **64** 頁的「**Reading 1 範例文章**」，並找出文章中舉例說明 **(illustrating)** 的用語。

解答·說明

你應該在以下段落中找到三個用語：

第二段：for example

第三段：… such as …/Take my country for example.

............................................................................................................................

☆ 請注意 for example 的標點符號，以及它在句子裡的位置應該是在例子清單的後面。

☆ 請注意 such as 的標點符號，以及它在句子裡的位置應該是例子清單的前面。

☆ 請注意 Take my country for example. 是一個完整的句子，後面接著一個軼聞或一個具體的案例。

　　我們來做一些練習，請聚焦於這些 set-phrases 的細節。

## ✎ Task 6

請把這些句子裡的錯誤加以改正。

1. Take for example that most people do not enjoy it.

　→ _____

2. A good example here is that Facebook is more popular with older people.

　→ _____

3. For example many people use it every day.

→ _____

4. It has many benefits such like it is easy to use.

→ _____

5. It has many features such as helping you to find people from your past.

→ _____

6. A good example here is Facebook which great popularity.

→ _____

7. In my situation when I was young I use Facebook to keep in touch with friends.

→ _____

解答・中譯

1. Take for example **the way** that most people do not enjoy it.
就舉例來說，大部分的人並不樂在其中。

2. A good example here is **the way** that Facebook is more popular with older people.
一個很好的例子是，臉書在較年長的人當中更受歡迎。

3. For example, many people use it every day.
例如，很多人是天天都使用。

4. It has many benefits ~~such~~ like it is easy to use.
它有很多好處，像是容易使用。

5. It has many features, such as helping you to find people from your past.
它有很多功能，諸如幫忙你找到過去認識的人。

6. A good example here is Facebook which **has** great popularity.
一個很好的例子是大受歡迎的臉書。

7. In my situation when I was young I **used** Facebook to keep in touch with friends.
以我的情況來說，我年輕時都是用臉書來跟朋友保持聯繫。

**Task 7**

請回到 **Task 1**，以舉例說明的用語將句子 **A**、**K**、**C** 用於闡述主題句。來看看範例。

> **EX.** Smoking is bad for your health. Not only that, but also it is bad for the health of the people around you. *A good example here is the way that smoking causes shortness of breath and high blood pressure*

1. Exercise is good for your physical health. Another good thing about exercise is that it is good for your mental health. _____

2. The arts teach us how to be true to ourselves. In addition to this, they teach us how to be good citizens. _____

_____

3. Social media has many benefits. Also, it is very popular. _____

_____

---

解答・中譯

請研讀我的範例，並確定你了解它們是怎麼寫出來的。

EX. 抽菸對你的健康有害。不僅如此，它還對你周遭眾人的健康有害。一個很好的例子就是，抽菸會造成呼吸急促和高血壓。

1. Exercise is good for your physical health. Another good thing about exercise is that it is good for your mental health. *For example, it makes you feel happy.*
運動對你的身體健康有益。運動的另一個好處在於，它也對你的心理健康有益。例如它會讓你覺得快樂。

2. The arts teach us how to be true to ourselves. In addition to this, they teach us how to be good citizens. *A good example here is the way that the theatre unites the individual with society because we are part of an audience.*
藝術教會我們要如何忠於自己。除此之外，它還教我們要怎麼當個好公民。一個很好的例子就是，戲劇會把個人與社會凝聚起來，因為我們是觀眾的一分子。

3. Social media has many benefits. Also, it is very popular. *A good example here is Facebook, which is the most popular social media site for my generation.*
社群媒體有很多好處。而且，它非常普及。Facebook 就是一個很好的例子，它是我們這一代最受歡迎的社群媒體網站。

我們來看一些英文寫作的眞題範例。

## 📝 Extra Practice Essays

利用前面學過的重點，練習針對以下題目來寫短文。請聚焦於舉出具體例子以闡述主題。

**TOPIC 1** 108 年學士後中醫（慈濟）

### IV. Composition.

Most doctors prefer to practice medicine in urban areas, but patients in rural areas need and deserve good professional medicine as much as those in urban areas. Please write an essay around 200-250 words to discuss the gap, in economic and cultural terms, between city and country in the practice of medicine, specifically, Chinese medicine. How do you think we should minimize the gap between city and country in the practice of Chinese medicine? That is, how should we make the practice of Chinese medicine between city and country more equitable?

**TOPIC 2** 107 年學士後中醫（慈濟）

### V. Composition: 20 分

Laws in most places prohibit terminally ill patients from choosing death and physicians from assisting them. Do you agree or disagree with it. Please write an essay around 200-250 words to explain your point of view and your arguments concerning this topic.

在你結束這個單元之前，請將下列的清單看過，確定你能將所有要點都勾選起來。如果有一些要點你還搞不清楚，請回頭再次研讀本單元的相關部分。

☐ 我知道如何透過一些具體例子來闡述主題句。

☐ 我學到了一些用於舉例說明的 set-phrases

☐ 我確實知道在使用 set-phrases 時，所要避免的一些常見錯誤。

☐ 我已經練習過如何使用這些 set-phrases。

☐ 我看到了一些真題範例，並針對那些題目練習寫了文章。

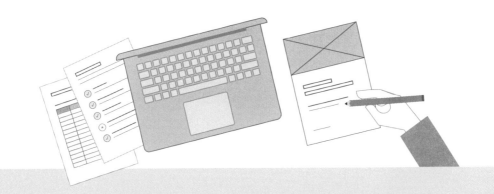

# Unit 9

## 如何對比主題句
### How to Contrast the Topic Sentence

在本單元裡,你會學到要如何運用對比或提出相反的
觀點來闡揚主題句。

首先來做一個練習：

### ✎ Task 1

**根據主題句，選出可作為對比意見的句子。**

EX. 主題句 Smoking is bad for your health.
對比意見 ___H___

1. 主題句 Exercise is good for your physical health.
   對比意見 _____

2. 主題句 The arts teach us how to be true to ourselves.
   對比意見 _____

3. 主題句 Social media has many benefits.
   對比意見 _____

A Exercise makes you feel happy.

B Exercise often hurts and can cause physical problems.

C Facebook is the most popular social media site for my generation.

D It is also good for your mental health.

E It is bad for the health of the people around you.

F It is very popular.

G Smoking causes shortness of breath and high blood pressure.

H Smoking is very enjoyable and helps to relax people.

I Social media has many dangers.

J The arts simply help us to pass the time and they have no usefulness.

K The theatre unites the individual with society because we are part of an audience.

L They teach us how to be good citizens.

1. B　2. J　3. I

☆ 請注意，正確的解答都是針對前一句話來提出相反的資訊。

## ✏ Task 2
請研究表格裡的用語、例句及下方的說明。

| contrasting ideas |
|---|
| • However, 不過 |
| • While it is true that v.p., nonetheless, v.p.<br>儘管 v.p. 為真，可是 v.p. |
| • While this may be true to some extent, nonetheless, v.p.<br>這在某種程度上或許為真，可是 v.p. |
| • On the other hand, 另一方面 |
| • Still, 話雖如此 |
| • On the contrary, 恰恰相反的是 |
| • Although v.p., v.p. 雖然 v.p.，但 v.p. |
| • By contrast, 相形之下 |
| • Then again, 然而 |

| sample sentences |
|---|
| • Smoking is very bad for the health. However, many people still smoke in spite of this knowledge.<br>抽菸對健康非常有害。不過儘管知道這點，很多人還是照抽。 |
| • While it is true that social media keeps us connected, nonetheless, it is also very isolating as well.<br>儘管社群媒體確實讓我們保持了連結，可是它同樣也讓人非常孤立。 |
| • Although exercise is generally good for you, there are some forms of exercise which must be done carefully.<br>雖然運動普遍來說對你有益，但有一些形式的運動做起來必須非常小心。 |

UNIT
9

☆ 注意，on the other hand 是一個慣用語，所以你不能對它進行任何改變。例如不能寫成 on the other side 或是 on the other foot。

☆ 在使用這些用語時，你必須非常了解 n.p. 和 v.p.。

☆ 使用 Although 時請留意，你絕對不可以在從屬子句裡使用它。

接下來的練習，請聚焦於 set-phrases 的細節。

## ✎ Task 3

請將下列各句中的字詞重組成語意正確的句子。

> **EX.** While smoking is that is it people bad it for you, many nonetheless, true enjoy
>
> _While it is true that smoking is bad for you, nonetheless, many people enjoy it_

1. While may be to nonetheless this some extent true social has disadvantages many media

_____

2. On other the hurt exercise hand can

_____

3. On many the people exercise don't enjoy contrary

_____

4. Although has not many it benefits exercise like people many do doing

_____

解答・中譯

EX. 雖然抽菸對健康有害是事實，可是很多人卻樂在其中。

1. While this may be true to some extent, nonetheless, social media has many disadvantages.

   雖然在某種程度上這或許是真的，可是社群媒體有很多缺點。

2. On the other hand, exercise can hurt.

   另一方面，運動可能會引發受傷。

3. On the contrary, many people don't enjoy exercise.

   恰恰相反的是，很多人並不喜歡運動。

4. Although exercise has many benefits, many people do not like doing it.

   雖然運動有很多好處，但很多人並不喜歡運動。

現在來看 set-phrases 的一些常見錯誤。

## ✏ Task 4

**請仔細研讀這些常見錯誤。**

❌ 錯誤

❖ Skydiving is a great sport with great benefits. On the other <u>side</u>, you need a lot of expensive equipment.

❖ The arts are very expensive to support. While this may be true, nonetheless, <u>great benefits</u>.

❖ <u>Although</u> everyone enjoys listening to music, <u>but</u> not many people are prepared to pay a lot of money for doing so.

✔ 正確

❖ Skydiving is a great sport with great benefits. On the other <u>hand</u>, you need a lot of expensive equipment.

❖ The arts are very expensive to support. While this may be true, nonetheless, <u>there are great benefits</u>.

❖ <u>Although</u> everyone enjoys listening to music, not many people are prepared to pay a lot of money for doing so.

請仔細閱讀第 **64** 頁的「**Reading 1 範例文章**」，並找出文章中用來對比 **(contrasting)** 的用語。

解答・說明

你應該在各個段落中找到四個用語：

引言：However, / while this may be true to some extent, nonetheless.

第二段：However

第三段：Although

..........................................................................................................

☆ 請注意，在引言裡這兩個用語是在一起的：However, while this may be true to some extent, nonetheless,

☆ 請特別注意有 although 的句子，裡面沒有 but。

我們來做一些練習，請聚焦於這些 set-phrases 的細節。

✐ **Task 6**

請把這些句子裡的錯誤加以改正。

1. Although many people want to quit smoking, but it is hard to do so.

→ _____

2. On the other side, some people believe the arts are not important.

→ _____

3. On the contrast regular exercise has been proved to be good for you.

→ _____

4. Many people have tried, however not everyone can succeed.

→ _____

5. While it is true that pleasant smoking, nonetheless, the health dangers are well known.

    → _____

6. While this may be true to an extent, but I do not think this is important.

    → _____

7. In contrast exercise is beneficial

    → _____

解答・中譯

1. Although many people want to quit smoking, ~~but~~ it is hard to do so.
   雖然很多人想要戒菸，但做起來很難。

2. On the other hand, some people believe the arts are not important.
   另一方面，有些人認為藝術並不重要。

3. On the contrary, regular exercise has been proved to be good for you.
   恰恰相反的是，規律運動證明是對你有益的。

4. Many people have tried. However, not everyone can succeed.
   很多人都試過。不過，並不是每個人都能成功。

5. While it is true that smoking is pleasant, nonetheless, the health dangers are well known.
   雖然抽菸的確令人愉快，可是其對健康的危害眾所皆知。

6. While this may be true to some extent, nonetheless, I do not think this is important.
   雖然這在某種程度上或許為真，但我認為這並不重要。

7. By contrast, exercise is beneficial.
   相形之下，運動則是有好處。

**Task 7**

請回到 **Task 1**，用對比意見的用語將句子 **B、J、I** 加入。來看看範例。

> **EX.** Smoking is bad for your health. Not only that, but also it is bad for the health of the people around you. _However, smoking is very enjoyable and helps to relax people_.

1. Exercise is good for your physical health. Another good thing about exercise is that it is good for your mental health.

   _____

2. The arts teach us how to be true to ourselves. In addition to this, they teach us how to be good citizens.

   _____

3. Social media has many benefits. Also, it is very popular.

   _____

解答・中譯

請研讀我的範例，並確定你了解它們是怎麼寫出來的。

EX. 抽菸對你的健康有害。不僅如此，它還對你周遭眾人的健康有害。然而，抽菸非常有樂趣，並有助於讓人放鬆。

1. _While it is true that_ exercise is good for your physical health, _nonetheless, there are some sports which can be very dangerous_.
   儘管運動對你的身體健康確實有益，可是有一些運動可能會非常危險。

2. The arts teach us how to be true to ourselves. In addition to this, they teach us how to be good citizens. _Still, the arts simply help us to pass the time and they have no usefulness_.
   藝術教會我們要如何忠於自己。除此之外，它還教我們要怎麼當個好公民。話雖如此，藝術就只是在幫助我們打發時間，並沒有用處可言。

3. Social media has many benefits. Also, it is very popular. *Then again, social media has many dangers*.

社群媒體有很多好處。而且，它非常普及。然而，社群媒體有許多危險之處。


我們來看一些英文寫作的真題範例。

## 📝 Extra Practice Essays

利用前面學過的重點，練習針對以下題目來寫短文。請聚焦於提出對比的資訊。


**TOPIC 1** 106 年學士後中醫（慈濟）

> **V. English Essay Writing. (20%) Use no more than 250 words.**
> **Background**: People live longer now than they used to. Discuss the causes of the increased longevity. Use examples and details to support the causes. Make sure that you have an introduction paragraph, one or more body paragraph(s), and a conclusion paragraph.

**TOPIC 1** 105 年學士後中醫（慈濟）

> **IV. Composition**: Express your ideas in no more than 250 words. 20%
> Discuss the importance of preventive medicine and effective ways to promote it.

在你結束這個單元之前，請將下列的清單看過，確定你能將所有要點都勾選起來。如果有一些要點你還搞不清楚，請回頭再次研讀本單元的相關部分。

□ 我知道如何針對主題句提出對比意見。

□ 我學到了一些用於舉例說明的 set-phrases

□ 我確實知道在使用 set-phrases 時，所要避免的一些常見錯誤。

□ 我已經練習過如何使用這些 set-phrases。

□ 我看到了一些眞題範例，並針對那些題目練習寫了文章。

閱讀以下寫作題目及範例文章。請留意兩個正文段落之主題句，你能不能看出這兩句是如何最為概括，以及段落中的其他各句是如何發展或對主題句提供具體的細節？

閱讀題目

> Global overpopulation is a serious problem which will get worse in the future.
> What are some of the problems, and what can individuals and governments do to solve them?

範例文章

The global population currently stands at around 7.5 billion. There is no doubt that this is a serious problem. This essay will look at some of the common problems caused by overpopulation and will then suggest two solutions.

One of the most serious problems is scarcity of resources. Food, clean water and agricultural land is fast running out due to overpopulation. We live on a finite planet, but we live as though we have unlimited resources at our disposal. A large and growing population causes environmental damage and pollution. The destruction of rainforests and other natural habitats to create enough land for agricultural use is the result of the pressure of a large population and the necessity to provide enough food for everyone. The earth's resources are being used up faster as a result of our expectation that every person on the planet can have a first world lifestyle.

In my opinion, the main solution to this problem is birth control, which should be encouraged by individuals and governments. This may cause some people to miss out on having a large family, but individuals should not think that having large families is a human right. Not only individuals but also governments have to act. Single and childfree people should be given tax concessions, and people with large families should be penalised by the government. The result of this will be a slowdown in the rate of population growth.

In the last analysis, if we are all going to share this planet in the future, we will need to be less selfish about our desires and expectations.

中譯

全球人口過剩是一個未來會惡化的嚴重問題。
其中的一些問題是什麼,而個人和政府能做些什麼來加以解決?

全球的人口目前約莫來到了 75 億。無庸置疑的是,這是個嚴重的問題。本文將會探討一些由人口過剩所造成的常見問題,然後建議兩個解決方案。

其中一個最嚴重的問題是資源匱乏。糧食、淨水和農地正快速耗竭,便是肇因於人口過剩。我們是住在有限的星球上,過起來卻彷彿是有無限的資源可支配。龐大且不斷增長的人口造成了環境損害和污染。為了開闢足夠的農業用地而去破壞雨林和其他的天然棲地,是導因於人口龐大和必須為大家提供足夠糧食的壓力。地球資源正以更快的速度耗盡,則是我們期望地球上的每個人都能過著第一世界生活方式的結果。

依我之見,解決這個問題的主要方法是控制生育,這需要個人和政府的支持與鼓勵。這樣或許會造成某些人無緣擁有大家庭,但個人不該認為擁有大家庭是人權。不僅是個人,政府也必須採取行動。單身和無子女的人應該要獲得稅金減免,有大家庭的人則該受到政府開罰。這樣的結果就會是減緩人口增長的速率。

歸根結底來說,假如我們未來全都要共享這個星球,我們就需要在慾望和期待上少點私心。

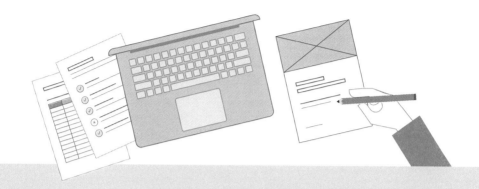

# Unit 10

## 如何寫原因
**How to Write about Reason**

這個單元的學習重點是用來描述狀況或問題之原因 (reason) 的用語。

寫作 problem/solution 類型的文章時，我們經常會提出造成問題的原因。在現實生活中，原因 (reason) 總是出現在狀況之前，它是狀況的成因。然而，我們陳述它們之間的關係時，未必會依照實際生活的關係。在中文，原因出現在動作或狀況之前——在中文裡，我們常以「由於」作爲句子開頭。但是在英文裡，更常見的寫法是把動作或狀況放在前面，然後才描述它的成因。

| 現實生活 |
| :---: |
| overpopulation　→　scarce resources<br>【原因】　　　　　【狀況】 |
| **中文** |
| overpopulation　→　scarce resources<br>【原因】　　　　　【狀況】 |
| **英文** |
| scarce resources　→　overpopulation<br>【狀況】　　　　　【原因】 |

　　在英文裡，我們會在主要子句（第一個子句）描述狀況，然後把狀況的成因放在從屬子句（第二個子句）。例如：Resources are scarce now because of overpopulation.

### ✏ Task 1

**請將左邊的「狀況」與右邊的「原因」進行配對。**

| 狀況 |
| :--- |
| Overpopulation has happened |
| Unemployment has increased in the developing world |

| 原因 |
| :--- |
| now most people can afford to buy a car |
| the internet |

| | |
|---|---|
| People are becoming more anti social | the rise of automation |
| Traffic congestion is getting worse | everyone is watching their smartphone screen all the time |
| Obesity is on the rise | there has been an increase in life expectancy among all ages. |
| It's now easier to share information | our sedentary lifestyle |

解答・說明

查看我在下方的解答，並確保你能了解其中的因果關係。

☆ 留意到最後一則適用於 argument/opinion 短文。

| 狀況 | 原因 |
|---|---|
| Overpopulation has happened<br>人口過剩發生了 | there has been an increase in life expectancy among all ages<br>所有年齡的預期壽命都有所增加 |
| Unemployment has increased in the developing world<br>開發中國家的失業人數增加 | the rise of automation<br>自動化興起 |
| People are becoming more anti social<br>人們變得更加反社會 | everyone is watching their smartphone screen all the time<br>每個人都是一直盯著智慧型手機的螢幕看 |
| Traffic congestion is getting worse<br>交通堵塞越來越嚴重 | now most people can afford to buy a car<br>現在大部分的人都買得起車子 |
| Obesity is on the rise<br>肥胖有增無減 | our sedentary lifestyle<br>我們習於久坐的生活方式 |
| It's now easier to share information<br>現在要分享資訊較為容易 | the internet<br>網際網路 |

現在，我們要看看可以使用哪些用語描述一個狀況或問題的原因。來看一些語塊。

✏ **Task 2**

**請研究表格裡的用語、例句和下方的說明。**

| reason |
| --- |
| • … because v.p. …　因為 v.p. |
| • … as v.p. …　是由於 v.p. |
| • … since v.p. …　是起因於 v.p. |
| • … because of n.p. …　是因為 n.p. |
| • … due to n.p. …　是肇因於 n.p. |
| • … due to the fact that v.p. …　由於事實是 v.p. |
| • … v.p. as a result of n.p. …　v.p. 是導因於 n.p. |
| • … n.p. is the result of n.p. …　n.p. 是 n.p. 的結果 |

| sample sentences |
| --- |
| • The forest has been cleared because the company wanted to use the land to raise cattle.<br>森林已經被砍伐，因為公司想用這片土地來養牛。 |
| • The water has been polluted due to the waste from the nearby factory.<br>水遭到了污染是肇因於附近工廠的廢水。 |
| • The infant mortality rate has decreased since the introduction of universal healthcare.<br>自從實施全民醫療保健以來，嬰兒死亡率已經降低。 |

☆ 在每一個句子裡，你會看到狀況先出現，接著是造成該狀況的原因。

☆ 注意，你絕對不可以在同一個句子裡使用 so 和 because。

☆ 即使 as a result of 和 is the result of 都用了 result 這個字，但它們實際的意思是在講原因，不要被搞混了。你使用它們的方式，應該和使用 because of 一模一樣，而且它們的意思都一樣。

☆ 注意，在 is the result of 的前面，絕對不可以用 v.p.。

☆ 請留意 is the result of 和 as a result of 之間的細微差異。

☆ 需特別注意哪些字後面接 n.p.，以及哪些字後面接 v.p.。

接下來我們來做一個練習，好讓你聚焦於語塊 (chunks) 的細節。

### ✎ Task 3

請將下列各句中的字詞重組成語意正確的句子。

1. The have deforestation cut of down trees been because.

2. Natural are industrialization being habitats to destroyed due

3. The is due river the discharge fact that polluted to it factories their into waste

4. The is deforestation disappearing as result rainforest a of

5. Soil is deforestation the of erosion result.

解答・中譯

1. The trees have been cut down because of deforestation.
   樹木遭到了砍伐是因為開墾森林之故。

2. Natural habitats are being destroyed due to industrialization.
   自然棲地正遭到破壞是肇因於工業化。

3. The river is polluted due to the fact that factories discharge their waste into it.
   河川遭到污染是由於工廠把廢水排放到裡面的這個事實。

4. The rainforest is disappearing as a result of deforestation.

雨林正在消失是導因於森林砍伐。

5. Soil erosion is the result of deforestation.

土壤受到侵蝕是導因於森林砍伐。

現在來看 chunks 的一些常見錯誤。

## ✏ Task 4

**請仔細研讀這些常見錯誤。**

---

❌ 錯誤

❖ As the company wanted to raise cattle, the forest was cleared.

❖ Because extreme weather is increasing, so people are afraid of living near the sea.

❖ People are getting fatter due to they have too much sugar in their diet.

❖ People are getting fatter is the result of too much sugar in their diet.

---

✅ 正確

❖ The forest was cleared as the company wanted to raise cattle.

❖ People are afraid of living near the sea because extreme weather is increasing.

❖ People are getting fatter due to the fact that they have too much sugar in their diet.

❖ Increased obesity is the result of too much sugar in people's diet.

請仔細閱讀第 **97** 頁的「**Reading 2 範例文章**」，並找出文章中用來描述原因的用語。

解答・說明

你應該在第二段落中找到三個用語：

• due to

• is the result of

• as a result of

☆ 注意，在每個句子中，第一個子句描述狀況，第二個子句描述狀況的原因。

☆ 注意 n.p. 的使用，due to 的後面不能接 v.p.。

## Task 6

請把這些句子裡的錯誤加以改正。

1. Resources are scarce because of there are too many people.

   → _____

2. Because the climate is heating, so there is extreme weather.

   → _____

3. As climate heating, there is extreme weather.

   → _____

4. Due to the temperature is high, there are many forest fires.

   → _____

5. Climate change as a result of burning fossil fuels.

   → _____

6. Climate change happens is the result of burning fossil fuels.

→ _____

7. The forest was destroyed due to the fact that raise cattle.

→ _____

解答・中譯

1. Resources are scarce because ~~of~~ there are too many people.
資源匱乏是因為人太多了。

2. **There is extreme weather because the climate is heating.**
會有極端天氣是因為氣候正在變暖。

3. As **the** climate **heats** there is extreme weather.
隨著氣候變暖，便會有極端天氣。

4. **There are many forest fires due to the high temperature.**
會有很多森林火災是肇因於高溫。

5. Climate change **happens** as a result of burning fossil fuels.
氣候變遷會發生是導因於燃燒化石燃料。

6. Climate change ~~happens~~ is the result of burning fossil fuels.
氣候變遷是燃燒化石燃料的結果。

7. The forest was destroyed due to the fact that **they wanted to** raise cattle.
森林遭到破壞要歸因於他們想要養牛這個事實。

---

✏ Task 7

請用描述原因的用語來寫作與 Task 1 中的「狀況」有關的句子。

> **EX.** *Overpopulation has happened because there has been an increase in life expectancy among all ages.*
> 人口過剩的發生是因為，所有年齡的預期壽命都有所增加。

解答・中譯

請研讀我的範例，並確定你了解它們是怎麼寫出來的。

1. Unemployment has increased in the developing world because of the rise of automation.

   開發中國家的失業人數增加是因為自動化的興起。

2. People are becoming more anti-social due to the fact that everyone is watching their smartphone screen all the time.

   人們正變得更加反社會，因為每個人都是一直盯著自己的智慧型手機螢幕看。

3. It's now easier to share information as a result of the internet.

   現在要分享資訊較為容易是因為有網際網路。

4. Traffic congestion is getting worse because now most people can afford to buy a car.

   交通堵塞越來越嚴重是因為現在大部分的人都買得起車子。

5. Rising obesity is the result of our sedentary lifestyle.

   肥胖有增無減是我們習於久坐的生活方式造成的。

我們來看一些英文寫作的真題範例。

 **Extra Practice Essays**

利用前面學過的重點，練習針對以下題目來寫短文。請聚焦於描述原因。

**TOPIC 1** 104 年學士後中醫（慈濟）

> **IV. English Composition (20%) Write your ideas in no more than 250 words.**
>
> The smart phone is getting so popular that it is almost a necessity for modern people. Despite its popularity, some people are still reluctant to get a smart phone. In your viewpoints, what are the reasons for NOT possessing and using a smart phone? Explain and elaborate your reasons and support your arguments.

二、作文題：**20 分**

Please write, in at least 300 words, a well-organized essay to express your opinion on "What causes people to seek non-Western medical cures like traditional Chinese medicine or herbal supplements?"

在你結束這個單元之前，請將下列的清單看過，確定你能將所有要點都勾選起來。如果有一些要點你還搞不清楚，請回頭再次研讀本單元的相關部分。

　　□ 我知道如何描述造成一個狀況或問題的原因。

　　□ 我學到了一些用於描述原因的語塊 (chunks)。

　　□ 我確實知道在使用語塊時，所要避免的一些常見錯誤。

　　□ 我已經練習過如何使用這些語塊。

　　□ 我看到了一些真題範例，並針對那些題目練習寫了文章。

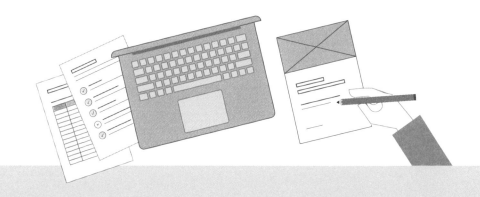

# Unit 11

## 如何寫結果
### How to Write about Result

前面學習過描述原因的用語,在本單元
要接著學習用來描述狀況或建議之結果
(result) 的用語。

使用描述結果的用語（及這種用語背後的觀念）的一個困難之處在於：什麼是原因，什麼又是結果，取決於你如何看待這件事，因為任何狀況都是前一個狀況的結果 (result)，也是下一個狀況的原因，所以這是某種因果關係鏈。一般在英文中的規則是，你必須把你想強調的資訊放在第一個子句。我們稱之為 topic position「主題位置」。

| 現實生活 |
|:---:|
| overpopulation　　→　　scarce resources<br>【原因】　　　　　　　　【結果】 |
| **英文（例句 1）** |
| scarce resources　　→　　overpopulation<br>【topic position 主題位置】　　【原因】 |
| **英文（例句 2）** |
| overpopulation　　→　　scarce resources<br>【topic position 主題位置】　　【結果】 |

例句 1 Resources will become scarce due to overpopulation.
資源會變得匱乏是由於人口過剩。

例句 2 Overpopulation is out of control. As a result, resources will become scarce.
人口過剩正在失控。因此資源會變得匱乏。

你可以從這兩個例子看到，透過更改放在 topic position「主題位置」的資訊，我們可以改變句子的重點，但整個句子的意思和現實生活的關係仍未改變。也就是在現實生活裡，人口過剩仍然是資源稀缺的原因，而不是相反的狀況。這樣你了解了嗎？

在 problem/solution 的文章裡，當你提出解決一個問題的方法，你也應該思考這個建議所產生的結果會是什麼。為了幫助你了解這一點，我們來進行一個練習。

請將左邊的「建議」與右邊的「結果」進行配對。

| 建議 | 結果 |
|---|---|
| The government should restrict the number of children each couple can have | a drop in obesity |
| Certain industries should be forbidden to automate | a slowdown in the unemployment rate |
| People should be encouraged to interact more with each other | communities will be stronger |
| There should be a very high tax on car sales | it's very difficult for governments and corporations to keep secrets |
| Physical exercise should be made a part of every schoolchild's day | reduce the number of cars on the road |
| The internet now reaches into most homes | the birthrate will go down |

解答・說明

查看下方的解答，並確保你能了解其中的因果關係。

☆ 注意，最後一個適合用在 argument/opinion 的文章。

| 建議 | 結果 |
|---|---|
| The government should restrict the number of children each couple can have<br>政府應該要對每對夫妻所能生下的子女數設限 | the birthrate will go down<br>生育率會下降 |
| Certain industries should be forbidden to automate<br>某些產業應該要禁止自動化 | a slowdown in the unemployment rate<br>失業率減緩 |

| | |
|---|---|
| People should be encouraged to interact more with each other<br>人們應該被鼓勵彼此有更多互動 | communities will be stronger<br>社區會更加強大 |
| There should be a very high tax on car sales<br>車輛銷售應該要課徵非常高額的稅 | reduce the number of cars on the road<br>減少路上的車輛數 |
| Physical exercise should be made a part of every schoolchild's day<br>身體鍛鍊應該要成為每位學童日常的一部分 | a drop in obesity<br>肥胖變少 |
| The internet now reaches into most homes<br>網際網路現在進入了大部分的家庭 | it's very difficult for governments and corporations to keep secrets<br>政府和企業非常難去保密 |

現在，我們來看看可使用哪些用語描述建議或解決方法將產生的結果。

## ✎ Task 2

請研究表格裡的用語、例句和下方的說明。

| result | |
|---|---|
| **certain** | **uncertain** |
| • … so…　於是<br>• This means that v.p.<br>　這意謂著 v.p.<br>• This will lead to n.p.<br>　這樣會導致 n.p.<br>• This may cause n.p.<br>　這樣或許會造成 n.p.<br>• The result of this will be n.p.<br>　這樣的結果將會是 n.p.<br>• The effect of this will be to V<br>　這樣的效應就會是 V | • This may cause s/o to V<br>　這樣或許會造成 s/o V<br>• This could lead to n.p.<br>　這樣可能會導致 n.p.<br>• This could result in n.p.<br>　這樣可能會導致 n.p.<br>• The result of this could be that v.p.<br>　這樣的結果可能會是 v.p.<br>• The effect of this could be to V<br>　這樣的效應可能會是 V |

| | |
|---|---|
| • As a result, v.p.<br>　因此，v.p. | • The effect of this could be n.p.<br>　這樣的效應可能會是 n.p. |
| • The result of this will be that v.p.<br>　這樣的結果會是 v.p. | • The result of this could be n.p.<br>　這樣的結果可能會是 n.p. |
| • This will result in n.p.<br>　這樣就會導致 n.p. | |
| • The effect of this will be n.p.<br>　這樣做的效果將是 n.p. | |

### sample sentences

• Universal healthcare was introduced, so infant mortality went down.
全民醫療保健被導入，於是嬰兒死亡率便下降了。

• Everyone has a smartphone now. As a result, it's easier for companies to target advertising.
現在每個人都有智慧型手機。因此公司較容易鎖定對象來打廣告。

• The government should give everyone a basic income. This will result in a fairer distribution of wealth.
政府應該給每個人基本收入。這樣就會形成更公平的財富分配。

• Parents should teach their children to be more polite. This could lead to a better society.
父母應該教育子女更有禮貌。這可能會帶來一個更美好的社會。

☆ 注意，so 表示結果。

☆ 務必留意 As a result（結果）和 Unit 10 中的 as a result of n.p. 還有 n.p. is the result of n.p.（原因）之間的差異，以及小詞之間的微小細節，例如逗點和大寫。

☆ This means that 和 so 更適合用在 argument / opinion 的文章裡。

☆ 這些 set-phrases 大部分是在一個句子的開始。所以你應該在第一個句子描述你的建議或解決方法，接著在下一個句子描述可能的結果。不要把它們寫成一個長的句子。

☆ 請注意，這裡的主詞常常是 this。你也可以用 that，但絕對不應該用 it。It 指的只有前一個句子的特定一個字，而 this 或 that 指的則是前面整個句子，或是前面句子的一組字。

我們來做習題，好讓你聚焦於 set-phrases 的細節。

## ✏ Task 3

下列各句中的第一個字是正確的，請將其後字詞重組成語意正確的句子。

1. This everyone means will enough have live that to on

   _____

2. This lead redistribution to will wealth greater

   _____

3. The of sure will be to effect on make enough to everyone this has live

   _____

4. This wealth will in result equality greater

   _____

5. This may people out to lose some cause

   _____

6. This in result could equality all for greater

   _____

7. The could of effect to ensure this be enough everyone that has

   _____

8. The of could this result universal be healthcare

   _____

9. The of this be could effect advertising more

   _____

1. This means that everyone will have enough to live on.
   這意謂著每個人都會得到足以維生之費用。

2. This will lead to greater wealth redistribution.
   這樣會促使財富重分配擴大。

3. The effect of this will be to make sure everyone has enough to live on.
   這樣做的效果將是確保每個人都得到足以維生之費用。

4. This will result in greater wealth equality.
   這樣就會導致更大的財富均等。

5. This may cause some people to lose out.
   這樣或許會造成某些人吃虧。

6. This could result in greater equality for all.
   這樣可能會使所有人更加平等。

7. The effect of this could be to ensure that everyone has enough....
   這樣的效應可能會是確保每個人都得到足夠的……

8. The result of this could be universal healthcare.
   這樣的結果可能會是全民醫療照護。

9. The effect of this could be more advertising.
   這樣的效應可能會是廣告變多。

現在來看 chunks 的一些常見錯誤。

## Task 4

**請仔細研讀這些常見錯誤。**

> ❌ 錯誤
>
> ❖ People should be prevented from living by the sea, as a result of they will not suffer so much from flooding.
>
> ❖ Governments should do more to help poor people, this could result in a drop in poverty.

- The laws against pollution should be more strictly enforced. It will lead to a better environment for everyone.
- Companies should enforce a lunchtime nap on their workers. This will lead to people will be more productive in the afternoon.

---

✅ 正確

- People should be prevented from living by the sea. As a result, they will not suffer so much from flooding.
- Governments should do more to help poor people. This could result in a drop in poverty.
- The laws against pollution should be more strictly enforced. This will lead to a better environment for everyone.
- Companies should enforce a lunchtime nap on their workers. This will lead to increased productivity in the afternoon.

---

## ✏️ Task 5

請仔細閱讀第 **97** 頁的 **Reading 2** 範例文章，並找出文章中用來描述原因的用語。

解答・說明

你應該在第三段中找到兩個用語：

- This may cause
- The result of this will be

........................................................................................

☆ 請注意，在每個句子裡，第一個子句是描述建議，第二個子句則描述建議可能產生的結果。

☆ 請注意 n.p. 和 v.p. 的使用。

## Task 6

請把這些句子裡的錯誤加以改正。

1. Companies should be more careful about the pollution they cause, this will lead to a better environment for everybody.

    → _____

2. There should be a tax on private cars. The result this will be less traffic on the roads.

    → _____

3. There should be a limit to the number of children a couple can have. This could lead a drop in the birth rate.

    → _____

4. People should spend less time looking at their smartphones.  The effect of this could be encourage more community feeling.

    → _____

5. People should be encouraged to walk more. The result of this could be that a drop in obesity.

    → _____

6. There should be more green spaces in the city. It will lead to a better quality of life for citizens.

    → _____

7. Advertising should be banned. This will result there will be less consumer spending.

    → _____

1. Companies should be more careful about the pollution they cause. **This** will lead to a better environment for everybody.

   公司應該要更加小心他們造成的污染。這樣會為每個人帶來更好的環境。

2. There should be a tax on private cars. The result **of** this will be less traffic on the roads.

   對私家車應該要加以課稅。這樣的結果就會是路上的車流變少。

3. There should be a limit to the number of children a couple can have. This could lead **to** a drop in the birth rate.

   一對夫妻所能生育的子女數應該要有所限制。這樣可能會促使生育率降低。

4. People should spend less time looking at their smartphones. The effect of this could be **to encourage** more community feeling.

   人們應該減少看智慧型手機的時間。這樣的效應可能會是鼓勵社區感提升。

5. People should be encouraged to walk more. The result of this could be ~~that~~ a drop in obesity.

   應該鼓勵人們多走路。這樣的結果可能會是肥胖變少。

6. There should be more green spaces in the city. **This** will lead to a better quality of life for citizens.

   城市裡應該要有更多的綠地。這樣會促使市民的生活品質更好。

7. Advertising should be banned. This will result **in** ~~there will be~~ less consumer spending.

   廣告應該要被禁絕。這樣就會促使消費者的花費減少。

---

## ✏ Task 7

請用描述結果的用語來寫作 Task 1 之相關建議。先看範例。

> **EX.** *The government should restrict the number of children each couple can have. As a result, the birthrate will go down.*
>
> 政府應該要限制每對夫妻所能生育的子女數。其結果就是生育率將會下降。

請研讀我的範例，並確定你了解它們是怎麼寫出來的。

1. Certain industries should be forbidden to automate. This could lead to a slowdown in the unemployment rate.
   某些產業應該要禁止自動化。這樣可能會促使失業率減緩。

2. People should be encouraged to interact more with each other. The result of this could be that communities will be stronger.
   人們應該被鼓勵彼此有更多互動。這樣的結果可能會是社區更加強大。

3. There should be a very high tax on car sales. The effect of this will be to reduce the number of cars on the road.
   車輛銷售應該要課徵非常高額的稅。這樣的效應就會是減少路上的車輛數。

4. Physical exercise should be made a part of every schoolchild's day. The effect of this could be a drop in obesity.
   身體鍛鍊應該要成為每位學童日常的一部分。這樣的效應可能會是肥胖變少。

5. The internet now reaches into most homes. This means that it's very difficult for governments and corporations to keep secrets.
   網際網路現在進入了大部分的家庭。這意謂著政府和企業非常難去保密。

我們來看一些英文寫作的真題範例。

 **Extra Practice Essays**

利用前面學過的重點，練習針對以下題目來寫短文。請聚焦於描述結果。

**TOPIC 1** 103 年學士後中醫（慈濟）

> **IV. Composition**: Express your ideas in no more than 250 words.
> **On Cosmetic Surgery**

二、作文題：**20** 分

The practitioners of traditional Chinese medicine (TCM) use herbal medicines, acupuncture, massage (tui na 推拿 ), and exercise (qi gong 氣功 ) to treat or prevent health problems. Which one of the four forms of TCM are you particularly interested in and why? Write at least 250 words to give reasons and examples for your answer.

在你結束這個單元之前，請將下列的清單看過，確定你能將所有要點都勾選起來。如果有一些要點你還搞不清楚，請回頭再次研讀本單元的相關部分。

□ 我知道如何表達一個建議將會產生的結果。

□我學到了一些 set-phrases 來兼而表達確定和不確定的結果。

□ 我確實知道在使用 set-phrases 時，所要避免的一些常見錯誤。

□ 我已經練習過如何使用這些 set-phrases。

□ 我看到了一些真題範例，並針對那些題目練習寫了文章。

閱讀以下寫作題目及範例文章。請留意兩個正文段落之主題句,你能不能看出這兩句是如何最為概括,以及段落中的其他各句是如何發展或對主題句提供具體的細節?

寫作題目

> Cybercrime–crime involving computers-is becoming more common as we put more of our personal information online.
> What are the problems associated with cybercrime, and what can be done to solve them?

範例文章

It cannot be denied that cybercrime is becoming more frequent. It's my opinion that this is a very serious problem that will only get worse in the future. This essay will look at some of the common problems and will then suggest two solutions.

It is becoming easier for criminals to access personal information for their own uses. Take for example the way that personal banking information is now all stored on the cloud. It is very easy for criminals to access this information and steal money from ordinary citizens' bank accounts. The financial industry should have foreseen this problem, and banks ought to have taken action to prevent this kind of crime. If banks were more careful about security, they wouldn't have this problem.

UNIT
**11**

The solution is to make banks and individuals responsible. Banks must be forced to improve their security systems so that hackers cannot access them. They should be made to refund any money stolen from their customers' accounts, and they ought to be forced to pay a fine when a theft occurs. If we force banks to be more careful about security, this kind of crime might not be so common. Another solution is to make customers more aware of the importance of changing their passwords frequently. If people change their passwords regularly, it will make it more difficult for criminals to access their information.

In conclusion, cybercrime causes great harm to private citizens and public institutions. Overall, it's clear that both banks and customers have a role to play in preventing it.

中譯

隨著我們將更多的個資放在網路上，網路犯罪──涉及電腦的犯罪──正變得越來越常見。與網路犯罪相關的問題有哪些，可以採取哪些措施來解決這些問題？

不容否認的是，網路犯罪正變得更為頻繁。我認為這是個非常嚴重的問題，未來只會變得更糟。本文將探討一些常見問題，然後提出解決方案。

犯罪分子要取得個資來為己所用變得越來越容易。以個人的銀行資訊現在全都是存放在雲端為例。犯罪分子很容易取得這些資訊，並從普通國民的銀行戶頭裡竊取款項。金融業早該預見這樣的問題，而銀行應當要採取行動來防範這類犯罪。如果銀行對安全方面更加謹慎，就不會有這樣的問題了。

解決方法則是讓銀行與個人負起責任。銀行必須強制改善安全系統，使駭客無法存取。對於顧客戶頭裡所遭竊的任何款項，它們都該加以退還，並且在竊案發生時，應當要強制繳交罰款。如果我們強制銀行在安全上更加小心，這種犯罪或許就不會那麼常見。另一個解決方法是讓顧客更加警覺頻繁更改密碼的重要性。如果人們定期更改密碼，犯罪分子要取得他們的資訊就會比較難。

總之，網路犯罪會對普通公民和公共機構造成重大的損害。整體而言，很清楚的是，銀行和客戶都可以在預防方面發揮作用。

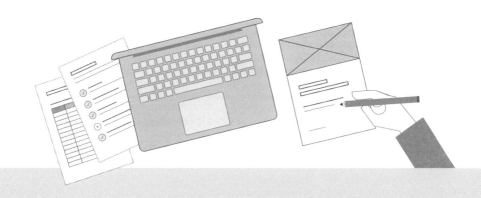

# Unit 12

## 如何用情態助動詞
## 來提出建議
### How to Use Modal Verbs to Make Suggestions

在這個單元裡,我們會學習要如何使用情態助動詞
(modal verbs) 來建議解決方法,以及要如何描述
在過去犯下錯誤所導致的問題。情態助動詞也可以
用在 argument/opinion 文章中來表達你的意見。

首先來看幾個情態助動詞的用法。

✎ Task 1

**請研究表格裡的用語、例句和下方的說明。**

| 非過去時間 | |
|---|---|
| **用語** | **意思和用法** |
| should V<br>shouldn't V<br>ought to V<br>ought not to V | 這些情態助動詞是用於表達現在或未來應該做卻還未做的事情。should 和 ought to 的意思及用法並沒有差異。它們都是用來提出建議。 |
| must V<br>mustn't V | 這個情態助動詞與 should 和 ought to 有非常相似的意思，但我們會用這個情態助動詞來表達對某個處境的急迫性。 |
| **例句** | |

- The government should impose fines for companies who pollute the environment.
  對於污染環境的公司，政府應該要處以罰款。

- There ought to be heavy fines for companies who break the law.
  對於違法的公司，理當要有巨額的罰款。

- Companies shouldn't think they can get away with breaking the law.
  公司不應該認為他們可以在違反法律的情況下逍遙法外。

- People ought not to be so selfish.
  人們不該這麼自私。

- We must act fast, otherwise it will be too late.
  我們必須盡速採取行動，否則就會太遲。

- We mustn't ignore this problem, otherwise future generations will never forgive us.
  我們不能忽視這個問題，否則子孫後代絕不會原諒我們。

☆ 所有例句都用現在或未來的時態來表達問題的解決方法。你可以在寫文章中的解決方法時使用這些用語。

☆ 請注意只有 ought 的後面接 to。人們常寫 must to，但這完全是錯的。如果你犯了這個錯誤，一定拿不到好分數。

☆ 請留意否定的形式，特別注意撇號的位置。

☆ shouldn't 和 mustn't 通常是縮寫，但 ought not to 通常不縮寫。

---

❌ 錯誤

❖ Governments <u>should to</u> listen to their people more.

❖ This problem <u>must'nt</u> be ignored.

❖ We <u>have to</u> take action now.

❖ Companies <u>oughtn't to</u> break the law.

---

✅ 正確

❖ Governments <u>should listen</u> to their people more.

❖ This problem <u>mustn't</u> be ignored.

❖ We <u>must</u> take action now.

❖ Companies <u>ought not to</u> break the law.

---

　　仔細看所有的例句你會發現，這些情態助動詞指涉的是現在、未來或是沒有指涉時間。因此，我們可以稱它們為 non-past modals「非過去情態助動詞」。你也可以用 should 和 ought to 來指涉過去，尤其是當你想要對過去的錯誤表達批判。在這種情況下，你必須加 have 和 past participle (p.p.)，也就是動詞的過去分詞。

**Task 2**

請研究表格裡的用語、例句和下方的說明。

| 過去時間 | |
|---|---|
| **用語** | **意思和用法** |
| should have p.p.<br>shouldn't have p.p.<br>ought to have p.p.<br>ought not to have p.p. | 這些情態助動詞用來表達對過去犯的錯誤之批判。 |
| **例句** | |

- The government should have acted sooner.
  = 它們太晚採取行動

- This company should not have broken the law.
  = 它們違法了

- The criminals ought to have received stricter punishments
  = 罪犯所受到的懲罰太輕

- They ought not to have committed the crime.
  = 他們犯了罪

☆ 所有例句都用來表達對過去所犯錯誤的批判。你可以在文章的問題部分使用這類用語。

☆ 必須用情態助動詞搭配 have + p.p. 來表達過去的時間。這表示你必須小心地使用正確的 p.p.，尤其當動詞是不規則動詞的時候。

☆ 請注意否定的 shouldn't have 是縮寫，但 ought not to 不用縮寫。

☆ 注意，你不應該用 must have p.p.，這樣寫的意思完全不一樣，不該在此使用。

> ❌ 錯誤
>
> ❖ He should <u>has</u> told his boss about the problem sooner.
>
> ❖ They shouldn't have <u>forgot</u> the regulations.
>
> ❖ The government <u>should'nt</u> have ignored the whistleblower.

❖ He should <u>have</u> told his boss about the problem sooner.

❖ They shouldn't have <u>forgotten</u> the regulations.

❖ The government <u>shouldn't</u> have ignored the whistleblower.

## ✏ Task 3

請仔細閱讀第 **121** 頁的 **Reading 3** 範例文章，並找出文章中使用到的情態助動詞。

解答・說明

第二段

• should have foreseen

• ought to have taken

第三段

• must be forced

• should be made to

• ought to be forced

☆ 注意，第二段中的情態助動詞全都是在指涉對過去時間行動的批評。

☆ 第三段的情態助動詞都指涉針對未來或現在時間的解決方法。

☆ 另外，請注意第三段的情態助動詞後面都接被動語態的不定詞：be forced、 be made to。

　　我們來練習這些情態助動詞。

## ✏ Task 4

下列各句的第一個字是正確的，請將其後字詞重組成語意正確的句子。

1. The companies who punish the government should severely pollute water.

2. Factories discharge the river ought been not allowed to to have their waste into.

_____

3. Traffic to ought be controls pollution and factory prevent controls implemented to air.

_____

4. Diesel banned ago cars should a long have been time.

_____

5. Whistleblowers by protected law be should.

_____

6. We must buying change our companies business so that polluting go habits out of.

_____

7. We must generations action think future take of and now.

_____

解答・中譯

1. The government should severely punish companies who pollute the water.
   對於造成水污染的公司，政府應該要加以嚴懲。

2. Factories ought not to have been allowed to discharge their waste into the river.
   不應任由工廠把廢水排進河裡。

3. Traffic controls and factory controls ought to be implemented to prevent air pollution.
   為了防止空氣污染，應該要實施車流控管和工廠控管。

4. Diesel cars should have been banned a long time ago.
   柴油車在很久以前就該被禁止。

5. Whistleblowers should be protected by law.
   吹哨者（告發人）應該要受到法律保護。

6. We must change our buying habits so that polluting companies go out of business.

我們必須改變購買習慣，好讓污染的公司倒閉。

7. We must think of future generations and take action now.

我們必須為子孫後代著想，並且現在就採取行動。

## ✎ Task 5

承上題，判斷各句分別指涉的是非過去時間還是過去時間。請在句子的旁邊為非過去時間寫 **NP**，過去時間寫 **P**。

解答

1. NP    2. P    3. NP    4. P    5. NP    6. NP    7. NP

## ✎ Task 6

請把這些句子裡的錯誤加以改正。

1. Factories should prevented from polluting the rivers.

_____

2. People ought to litter.

_____

3. People should'nt drive big polluting cars.

4. That polluting factory ought to have be closed a long time ago.

_____

5. The criminals should'nt have been allowed to go free.

_____

6. The regulations should had been enforced more strictly.

_____

7. There ought be stronger laws against polluters.

_____

8. They ought to have bought such a polluting car.

_____

9. We must to take action now otherwise it will be too late.

_____

10. We should have took action a long time ago. Now it is too late.

_____

解答・中譯

1. Factories should **be** prevented from polluting the rivers.
應該要防止工廠污染河川。

2. People ought **not** to litter.
民眾不應亂丟垃圾。

3. People **shouldn't** drive big polluting cars.
人們不該開污染大的車。

4. That polluting factory ought to have **been** closed a long time ago.
那座污染的工廠在很久以前就該關閉了。

5. The criminals **shouldn't** have been allowed to go free.
不應任由罪犯逍遙法外。

6. The regulations should **have** been enforced more strictly.
這些法規應該要更嚴格地執行。

7. There ought **to** be stronger laws against polluters.
應該要有更強的法律來對付污染者。

8. They ought **not** to have bought such a polluting car.
他們不該買這麼會污染的車。

9. We must ~~to~~ take action now otherwise it will be too late.
我們必須現在採取行動，否則就會太遲。

10. We should have **taken** action a long time ago. Now it is too late.
我們在很久以前就該採取行動了。現在太遲了。

　　請將正確的解答與 Task 1、Task 2 表格中的詞語做比較。務必使用完全正確的小詞，指涉過去時間的情態助動詞要用過去分詞，非過去時間的情態助動詞要用不定詞，以及省略符號要在正確的地方。另外，別忘了否定句裡要納入「not」。這些全都是常見錯誤。一定要特別留意！

　　最後來看一些英文寫作的真題範例。

## 📝 Extra Practice Essays

利用前面學過的重點，練習針對以下題目來寫短文。請聚焦於提出建議。

**TOPIC 1** 102 年學士後中醫（中國）

**VI. Composition**

Recently, hazardous additives have been identified in a great variety of foods in Taiwan. Write an essay of two paragraphs in 150-200 words discussing first why these substances were added and the consequences they have brought, and then what measures should be taken by the government, the industries, and the consumers.

**TOPIC 2** 102 年學士後中醫（義守）

**二、作文題：20 分**

The patient-doctor relationship has been and remains a keystone of care; however, deterioration of the patient-doctor relationship becomes a significant source of stress for doctors in Taiwan. Write at least 250 words to express the cause of the problem and discuss possible solutions toward this issue.

在你結束這個單元之前，請將下列的清單看過，確定你能將所有要點都勾選起來。如果有一些要點你還搞不清楚，請回頭再次研讀本單元的相關部分。

☐ 我知道如何用情態助動詞來表達問題的解決方法。

☐ 我學到了有些情態助動詞是在指涉過去，有些是在指涉非過去。

☐ 我確實知道在使用情態助動詞時所要避免的一些常見錯誤。

☐ 我已經練習過如何使用這些情態助動詞。

☐ 我看到了一些真題範例，並針對那些題目練習寫了文章。

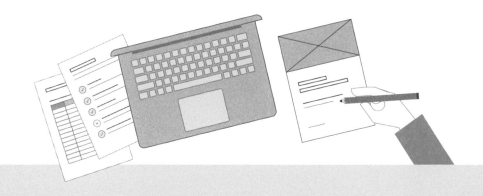

# Unit 13

## 如何使用條件句
**How to Use Conditionals**

在寫作時，你可能會想透過描述一個建議的條件
和後果以發展自己的主題句，此時可以運用兩種
條件句：the First Conditional「第一類條件句」和
the Second Conditional「第二類條件句」。在本單
元，我們要來看看它們的意思以及相關用語。

The First Conditional「第一類條件句」是指真實的條件。這表示如果第一個子句描述的情況真的發生了，第二個子句描述的情況也會自然成為第一句的結果而發生。你應該用這種條件句來描述在現實生活中，確實可能在現在或未來發生的情況。

### ✏ Task 1

請研究表格裡的例句和其下的說明。

| The First Conditional |
|---|
| • If I get a high score in my test, I will be admitted to study medicine.<br>　假如在測驗中拿到高分，我就會錄取去讀醫科。<br>• If the government enforces the law, fewer companies will break it.<br>　假如政府強力執法，違反的公司就會比較少。 |

☆ 這些都有真實的可能性。
☆ 只要句子第一個部分的條件成立了，句子第二部分也會自然發生而成為結果。
☆ 第一個句子表達只要你用功，你就沒有理由得不到高分。
☆ 第二個句子表達政府沒有理由無法執法。這些是在現實上有可能。

相反的，The Second Conditional「第二類條件」指的是某個狀況永遠都不會發生，因為它完全違背現實，因為它完全不是真實的。

### ✏ Task 2

請研究表格裡的例句和其下的說明。

| The Second Conditional |
|---|
| • If I got a high score in my test, I would be able to study medicine.<br>　假如在測驗中拿到高分，我就能去讀醫科了。<br>• If the government enforced the law, fewer companies would break it.<br>　假如政府強力執法，違反的公司就會比較少了。 |

☆ 這些句子是假設性或不真實的，完全違反現實。

☆ 第一個句子表達的是，你不打算去做測驗，你沒有去申請，你沒有意圖要為它去念書。

☆ 第二個句子表達的是，政府不會去強力執法，而且它們也不打算執法。

　　這裡很重要的是了解第一類和第二類條件句之間的差異，不在於時間，而在於現實性。如果你選擇寫第一類條件句，這表示你因為一些原因而相信條件有可能成真，它可能真的發生。如果你選擇第二類條件句，這表示你想要表達這個條件完全不可能成真，而且也完全不可能在現實發生。

　　既然了解了這兩類條件句的意思，我們就來看詞語。

## 第一類條件句 First Conditionals

### Task 3

**請研究表格、例句和其下的說明。**

| 真實 | |
|---|---|
| 條件子句 | 結果子句 |
| If v.p. (present simple), | (will/won't V)<br>(may/may not V)<br>(might/might not V)<br>(can V)<br>(will probably V …) |
| 例句 | |

- If there are more traffic police on the roads, motorists might drive more carefully.
  如果路上有更多交通警察，駕駛人或許就會開得更小心。

- Future generations will be in serious trouble if we continue to ignore climate change.
  如果我們繼續忽視氣候變遷，子孫後代就會面臨嚴重的麻煩。

- If the government introduces a higher road tax, fewer people will buy cars.
  如果政府採行較高的用路稅，買車的人就會比較少。
- If we don't do something about global warming now, future generations might not have a good life.
  如果我們現在不對全球暖化有所作為，後代子孫或許就不會有好的生活。

☆ 注意，所有句子都表達現在或未來可能成真的狀況。

☆ 所有句子都有兩個子句，而且如果句子用條件子句開頭，該句就會有逗號；如果用結果子句開頭，就沒有逗號。閱卷者會看這些小細節，所以請確保你寫得正確。

☆ 你必須在條件子句使用現在簡單式，並在結果子句使用 will 或其他情態助動詞。注意，絕對不能在條件子句用 will。

☆ 可以把結果子句放在前面，但如果你這樣做，請小心動詞時態。

☆ 注意你在結果子句可以用哪一個情態助動詞。may 和 might 表達句子裡描述的結果只是眾多可能性的其中一個，亦即還有其他可能性是你沒有描述的。

☆ 不要擔心 may 和 might 的差異，這些情態助動詞的意思和用法都相同。

---

❌ 錯誤

❖ If we take action <u>now it</u> won't be too late.

❖ If we <u>will</u> cut carbon emissions, it will help the environment.

---

✔ 正確

❖ If we take action <u>now, it</u> won't be too late.

❖ If we <u>cut</u> carbon emissions, it will help the environment.

---

✏ Task 4

請仔細閱讀第 121 頁的 Reading 3 範例文章，並找出文章中使用第一類條件句的例子。

第三段

- If we force banks to be more careful about security, this kind of crime might not be so common.
- If people change their passwords regularly, it will make it more difficult for criminals to access their information.

☆ 這個段落使用真實的 First Conditionals，表達這些事很容易發生。

## ✐ Task 5

**請把這些句子裡的錯誤加以改正。**

1. If we will not be careful, bad things will happen.

2. If we won't take action now, it could well be too late.

3. If the government won't do something about this problem, it gets worse.

4. If people will stop buying cars, there will be less traffic on the roads.

UNIT
**13**

5. Climate change will only get worse if we won't do something about it now.

解答・中譯

1. If we **are not** careful, bad things will happen.
   如果我們不小心，壞事就會發生。

2. If we **don't** take action now, it **may** well be too late.
   如果我們現在不採取行動，很有可能就會太遲了。

3. If the government **doesn't** do something about this problem, it **will just get** worse.

如果政府不對這個問題有所作為，它就會惡化下去。

4. If people ~~will~~ stop buying cars, there will be less traffic on the roads.

如果人們停止買車，路上的車流就會減少。

5. Climate change will only get worse if we **don't** do something about it now.

如果我們現在不有所作為，氣候變遷只會惡化下去。

☆ 注意不可以把 will 擺進 if 子句中，且 if 子句要用現在簡單式。

現在我們就來練習 First Conditionals。

## Task 6

請用 **Task 3** 中的用語擴展下方表格的資訊。來看看範例。

| 真實 | |
|---|---|
| 條件 | 結果 |
| government and individuals share responsibility | solve problem |
| put up speed cameras | reduce speeding |
| good education | find a better job |
| increase tax on fuel | people think twice before using private car |
| invest in renewable energy | less pollution |
| stop hunting whales | increase in whale population |

**EX.** *If government and individuals share their responsibility, together we can solve this problem.*

假如政府和個人共同負起責任，我們就能一起解決這個問題。

很顯然，我不會知道你寫了什麼，但請研究我的範例，並確定你了解它們是怎麼寫出來的。

1. If they put up speed cameras everywhere, this will reduce speeding.
   如果四處架設測速照相機，這樣就能減少超速。

2. If people have a good education, they can find a better job.
   如果人們受到好的教育，他們就能找到更好的工作。

3. If the government increases the tax on fuel, people might think twice before using private cars.
   如果政府對燃料增稅，民眾在使用私家車前或許就會三思。

4. There will be less pollution if the government invests more in renewable energy.
   如果政府在可再生能源上的投資更多，污染就會變少。

5. If we stop hunting whales now, there could be an increase in the whale population in a few years.
   如果我們現在停止捕鯨，過幾年後鯨魚的總數可能就會有所增加。

接下來，我們來練習 Second Conditionals。

## ⤵ 第二類條件句 Second Conditionals

### ✎ Task 7

請研究表格、例句和其下的說明。

| 非真實 | |
|---|---|
| 條件子句 | 結果子句 |
| If v.p. (past simple), | (would/wouldn't V)<br>(would probably V …)<br>(could V) |

- If people were not so greedy, they wouldn't consume so many of the earth's resources.
  假如民眾不要這麼貪心，就不會消耗掉地球這麼多的資源了。

- If corporations cared more about people and less about profits, they might not make so much money, but their employees would probably be happier.
  假如企業更關心的是人而不是利潤，它們所賺的錢或許不會這麼多，但員工可能會比較快樂。

- I could do more to prevent bad things from happening if I had more power.
  如果我有更大的權力，我就能做得更多來防止壞事發生了。

- If I didn't have Facebook, I would not be able to stay in touch with my parents so easily while I'm abroad.
  假如我沒有臉書，我在國外時就沒辦法這麼容易跟父母保持聯繫了。

---

☆ 所有句子都表達現在或未來不可能成真的狀況，亦即都與事實相反。也就是人們確實貪婪、企業不在乎人們等等。

☆ 和 First Conditional 句子一樣，所有句子都有兩個子句。而且如果句子用條件子句開頭，該句就有逗號；如果用結果子句開頭，就沒有逗號。

☆ 注意，你必須在條件子句使用過去簡單式。這點讓人很混淆。這裡的過去簡單式不是表示過去的時間，而是表示非真實的過去時間。過去簡單式有兩個意思：真實的過去時間，例如 I went, and I came back，以及非真實的過去時間，例如 If I went, I would never come back.。

☆ 此外，你在結果子句必須使用 would 和 wouldn't，但不能用 couldn't。然而在條件子句中則絕對不可以用 would。

☆ 你可以把結果子句放在前面，但如果你這樣做，請小心動詞時態。

---

❌ 錯誤

❖ If we all <u>obey</u> the laws, social problems <u>disappear</u>.

❖ If governments <u>would rule</u> for everyone, not just for a privileged few, our country <u>is</u> a better place.

正確

❖ If we all <u>obeyed</u> the laws, social problems <u>would disappear</u>.
❖ If governments <u>ruled</u> for everyone, not just for a privileged few, our country <u>would be</u> a better place.

## 📝 Task 8

請仔細閱讀第 **121** 頁的「**Reading 3 範例文章**」，並找出文章中使用第二類條件句的例子。

解答・說明

第二段

• If banks were more careful about security, they wouldn't have this problem.

............................................................

☆ 這句是非真實或第二類條件句。表達在現實裡，銀行並不在意它們的安全性（但應該要在意才對，所以它是與現實相反）。

## 📝 Task 9

請把這些句子裡的錯誤加以改正。

1. If we would take action now, we could solve this problem.

_____

2. If people wouldn't buy big polluting cars, we didn't have so much pollution in our cities.

_____

3. If the government decided to do something about it the situation would probably change.

_____

4. If I didn't have a smartphone, I couldn't be able to post pictures on Instagram.

_____

5. If we are more careful, accidents wouldn't happen.

_____

解答・中譯

1. If we **took** action now, we could solve this problem.
   如果我們現在採取行動，就能解決這個問題了。

2. If people **didn't** buy big polluting cars, we **wouldn't** have so much pollution in our cities.
   如果人們不買會造成污染嚴重的大型車，城市就不會有這麼多的污染了。

3. If the government decided to do something about it, the situation would probably change.
   若是政府決定對此採取行動，情況可能就會改變。

4. If I didn't have a smartphone, I **wouldn't** be able to post pictures on Instagram.
   如果我沒有智慧型手機，就沒辦法在 Instagram 上發布照片了。

5. If we **were** more careful, accidents wouldn't happen.
   如果我們更加小心，意外就不會發生了。

☆ 再提醒一次，不要把 would 擺進 if 子句裡，且在 if 子句裡要用過去簡單式。別忘了逗點。

現在我們就來練習 Second Conditionals。

✎ Task 10

請用 **Task 7** 中的用語擴展下方表格的資訊。來看看範例。

| 非真實 | |
|---|---|
| 條件 | 結果 |
| no media | people's general knowledge of world lower |

| government supply houses for everyone | high quality of living for all |
|---|---|
| no foreign workers in Taiwan | a lot of jobs not get done |
| I am prime minister | solve this problem |
| everyone is honest and not so selfish | social problems disappear |
| stop manufacturing cars | economy collapse |

**EX.** *If there were no media, people's general knowledge of the world would be a lot lower.*
如果沒有媒體，民眾對世界的概括認識就會少很多。

解答·中譯

再一次地，我顯然不會知道你寫了什麼，但請研究我的範例，並確定你了解它們是怎麼寫出來的。

1. If the government supplied houses for everyone, there would be a higher quality of living for all.
   如果政府供房給每個人，那麼所有人就會有更高的生活品質了。

2. A lot of jobs would not get done if there were no foreign workers living in Taiwan.
   如果沒有住在台灣的外籍移工，很多工作就會無法完成。

3. If I were/was prime minister, I would solve this problem immediately.
   如果我是總理，我就會立刻來解決這個問題。

4. If everyone was honest and not so selfish, a lot of social problems would disappear overnight.
   如果每個人都誠實而不要這麼自私，很多社會問題就會在一夕之間消失了。

5. If they stopped manufacturing cars, the economy of many countries would totally collapse.
   如果他們停止製造車輛，很多國家的經濟就會全部垮掉了。

UNIT
**13**

　　最後來看一些英文寫作的真題範例。

利用前面學過的重點，練習針對以下題目來寫短文。請聚焦於寫出條件句。

**TOPIC 1** 102 年學士後西醫（高醫）

> **IV. Essay Writing. 20 points**
>
> Please write in at least 200 words a well-organized essay to express your opinion on "Every obstacle is an opportunity." Do you agree or disagree with the statement above? Give specific reasons or examples to support your ideas.

**TOPIC 2** 101 年學士後中醫（義守）

> 二、作文題：**20 分** (Please discuss your ideas in at least 250 words.)
> Doctor-patient confidentiality refers to the promise that a doctor will not tell anyone else about a patient's health problems. Are there times when this confidentiality should be broken? Please express your opinion.

　　在你結束這個單元之前，請將下列的清單看過，確定你能將所有要點都勾選起來。如果有一些要點你還搞不清楚，請回頭再次研讀本單元的相關部分。

□ 我很清楚 First Conditionals「第一類條件句」和 Second Conditionals「第二類條件句」之間在意義和用法上的差異。

□ 我確實知道在使用條件句時所要避免的一些常見錯誤。

□ 我已經練習使用條件句。

□ 我看到了一些真題範例，並針對那些題目練習寫了文章。

# Reading 4
## sample essay: argument/opinion

閱讀以下寫作題目及範例文章。請留意兩個正文段落之主題句,你能不能看出這兩句是如何最為概括,以及段落中的其他各句是如何發展或對主題句提供具體的細節?

### 寫作題目

Many people believe that social networking sites (such as Facebook) have had a huge negative impact on both individuals and society.
To what extent do you agree.

### 範例文章

There are those who say that social networking sites have had a detrimental effect on individuals as well as society and local communities. On the other hand, while I believe that such sites are mainly beneficial to the individual, I agree that they have had a damaging effect on local communities. There are many reasons why I think so.

With regard to individuals, the impact that online social media has had on each individual person has clear advantages. Firstly, people from different countries are brought together through such sites as Facebook. Before the development of technology and social networking sites, which began to appear around the early 2000s, people rarely had the chance to meet or communicate with anyone outside of their immediate circles or community. Secondly, Facebook also has groups which offer individuals a chance to meet to participate in discussions with other people who share common interests.

On the other hand, the effect Facebook and other social networking sites have had on societies and local communities can only be seen as negative. Rather than individual people taking part in the local community, they are instead choosing to take more interest in people online. Consequently, the people within local communities are no longer forming close or supportive relationships. In addition, society as a whole is becoming increasingly disjointed and fragmented as people spend more time online with people they have never met face to face and with whom they will never meet in the future.

To sum up, although social networking sites have brought individuals closer together, they have not had the same effect on society or local communities. I firmly believe that local communities should do more to try and involve local people in local activities in order to promote the future of community life.

中譯

很多人相信，社交網站（諸如臉書）對個人與社會都產生了巨大的負面衝擊。
你贊同到什麼程度？

有人說，社交網站對個人、社會以及地方社區產生了不利影響。另一方面，我固然相信這類的網站主要是對個人有好處，但我也贊同它對地方社區產生了破壞性的影響。我為什麼會這麼想，理由有很多。

在個人方面，線上社群媒體對每位個別民眾的影響具有明顯的優點。首先，不同國家的人透過諸如臉書等的網站而牽連在一起。在約莫從 2000 年初開始出現的科技和社交網站發展起來前，人們鮮少有機會與就近的圈子或社群以外的任何人結識或交流。其次，臉書也有社群，為個人提供機會，與其他有共同興趣的人見面，參與討論。

另一方面，臉書和其他社交網站對社會與地方社區所產生的影響只能以負面視之。個別民眾不是去投入地方社群，而反倒是選擇對網上的人抱持較大的興趣。結局就是，地方社區裡的人不再形成緊密或支援的關係。此外，隨著人們花更多的時間在網上與他們從未見過面以及將來永遠不會見面的人在一起，整個社會正變得日益支離破碎。

總而言之，雖然社交網站拉近了人與人之間的距離，但對社會或地方社群卻沒有產生相同的影響。我堅信地方社區應該要做得更多，試著去把地方民眾帶進當地活動裡，以藉此促進社區生活的未來。

UNIT
13

## Notes

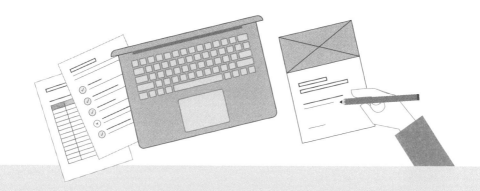

# Unit 14

## 如何運用動詞時態
### How to Use Verb Tenses

在這個單元中,我們將學習如何使用適當
的動詞時態以改善寫作,而這些時態的用
法則取決於你文章中所指涉的時間。

其實在寫作測驗中，你必須知道如何正確使用的動詞時態只有五種。

## ✏️ Task 1

請研讀表格及下方的例句，並將各句表達的意思分別屬於 **ABCDE** 哪一種時態寫在 （　）中。

| 時態與時間 | | |
|---|---|---|
| A | **present simple**<br>現在簡單式 | 這個時態是用來描述和時間無關的事情，例如：事實和意見。它也可以用在用來描述狀態的動詞，例如 be 和 have。 |
| B | **present continuous**<br>現在進行式 | 這個時態是用來描述在現在尚未結束的時間下，進行的趨勢或活動。如果沒有結果，或是你不想把重點放在結果上，請使用這種時態。 |
| C | **present perfect simple**<br>現在完成式 | 這個時態是用來描述在現在尚未結束的時間下，行動的結果。 |
| D | **past simple**<br>過去簡單式 | 這個時態是用來描述在過去已經結束的行動或狀態。 |
| E | **will V**<br>未來簡單式 | 請用 will V 來描寫你很確定未來會發生的行動或狀態。**但是，不要用 will 來寫習慣、事實或慣例。** |

1. （　） Many people died of the plague.
   很多人是死於瘟疫。

2. （　） The arts play a significant role in public life.
   藝術在公共生活中扮演了要角。

3. （　） The problem is getting worse all the time.
   這個問題一直在惡化。

4. （　） The situation will only get worse.
   情況只會變得更糟。

5. (　　) There has been a great improvement in living standards.
生活水準有了很大的提升。

6. (　　) The situation is very bad.
情況非常糟。

7. (　　) Alexander Fleming discovered penicillin in the 1940s.
亞歷山大‧傅雷明在 1940 年代發現了青黴素。

8. (　　) We are trying to do something about it.
我們正試著要有所作為。

9. (　　) The results so far have been very good.
到目前為止的結果非常好。

10. (　　) Climate change will only get worse.
氣候變遷只會惡化下去。

解答

1. D　2. A　3. B　4. E　5. C　6. A　7. D　8. B　9. C　10. E

## ✏ Task 2

請仔細閱讀第 **145** 頁的「**Reading 4 範例文章**」，把文章中所有動詞都畫上底線。接著，根據動詞時態填入下方表格的正確欄位。

| 動詞時態 | | | | |
|---|---|---|---|---|
| 無時間動詞 present simple | 現在時間動詞（活動或趨勢） present continuous | 現在時間動詞（結果） present perfect | 過去時間動詞 past simple | 未來時間動詞 will V |
|  |  |  |  |  |

| 動詞時態 | | | | |
|---|---|---|---|---|
| 無時間動詞<br>present simpl | 現在時間動詞<br>（活動或趨勢）<br>present<br>continuous | 現在時間動詞<br>（結果）<br>present perfect | 過去時間動詞<br>past simple | 未來時間動詞<br>will V |
| say<br>believe<br>are<br>agree<br>has<br>are brought<br>has<br>share<br>spend<br>can<br>should | are choosing<br>are forming<br>is becoming | have had<br>has had<br>have met<br>have brought | began<br>had | will meet |

## ✏ Task 3

請根據每個句子的提示，從上方動詞語庫中選出最適當的動詞及時態填入空格中。（有些動詞可能會使用不只一次）

| | | | | |
|---|---|---|---|---|
| be | become | discover | have | cause |
| increase | know | start | worsen | die |

1. Actors _____ highly developed skills. ▸ fact

2. Antibiotics _____ eventually _____ useless.
   ▸ future action/state

3. Climate change _____ a catastrophic effect on many lives around the world. ▸ present result

4. Climate change _____ a catastrophic effect on many lives around the world. ▸ trend

5. More people _____. ▸ future action

6. Scientists did not know what _____ the problem, until they _____ the virus. ▸ past actions

7. The gaming trend among young people _____. ▸ trend

8. The situation _____ in the last few years. ▸ present result

9. The situation _____ bad before the government _____ doing something about it. ▸ past state

10. The theatre industry in London _____ world famous. ▸ fact

---

解答・説明

1. Actors **have** highly developed skills.
   演員具備高度養成的技能。

2. Antibiotics **will** eventually **become** useless.
   抗生素終歸會變得毫無用處。

3. Climate change **has had** a catastrophic effect on many lives around the world.
   氣候變遷對全世界的許多生命產生了災難性的影響。

4. Climate change **is having** a catastrophic effect on many lives around the world.
   氣候變遷正對全世界的許多生命產生災難性的影響。

5. More people **will die**.
   更多的人會喪命。

6. Scientists did not know what **caused** the problem, until they **discovered** the virus.
   直到發現了這種病毒，科學家們才知道問題是由什麼所造成。

UNIT
14

7. The gaming trend among young people **is increasing**.
   年輕人的遊戲趨勢正在上升。

8. The situation **has worsened** in the last few years.
   情況在過去幾年來惡化了。

153

9. The situation **was** bad before the government **started** doing something about it.

   在政府開始有所作為前，情況都很惡劣。

10. The theatre industry in London **is** world famous.

    倫敦的劇場業是舉世聞名的。

最後來看一些英文寫作的眞題範例。

## 📝 Extra Practice Essays

利用前面學過的重點，練習針對以下題目來寫短文。請聚焦於動詞時態。

**TOPIC 1** 101 年學士後中醫（中國）

> **VI. Composition**: Write an essay of two paragraphs in 150-200 words. Describe an experience of yours or your friends with **stray dogs** in the first paragraph. Then comment on the issue of stray dogs in the second paragraph.

**TOPIC 2** 108 年學士後中醫（慈濟）

> **IV. Composition**
>
> Most doctors prefer to practice medicine in urban areas, but patients in rural areas need and deserve good professional medicine as much as those in urban areas. Please write an essay around 200-250 words to discuss the gap, in economic and cultural terms, between city and country in the practice of medicine, specifically, Chinese medicine. How do you think we should minimize the gap between city and country in the practice of Chinese medicine? That is, how should we make the practice of Chinese medicine between city and country more equitable?

在你結束這個單元之前，請將下列的清單看過，確定你能將所有要點都勾選起來。如果有一些要點你還搞不清楚，請回頭再次研讀本單元的相關部分。

□ 我確實學會五種在寫作時可使用的不同動詞時態。

□ 我看到了這些動詞時態在上下文裡的很多例子。

□ 我已經練習去使用了正確的動詞時態。

□ 我看到了一些真題範例，並針對那些題目練習寫了文章。

Notes

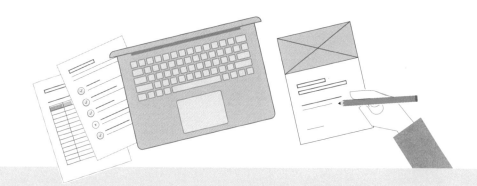

# Unit 15

## 如何寫結語
### How to Write a Conclusion

英文寫作的開頭再好，也必須搭配能讓閱卷者眼睛一亮的精彩結尾才能拿到高分。在本書最後，我們就要來學習如何寫出好的「結語」。

基本上，寫結論非常簡單。你最多只需要用一句或兩句寫結語。這裡有一張清單可以協助你。

---

### 寫作「結語」的清單

1. 用一個句子總結你的論證
2. 重申你的意見
3. 保持概括性
4. 不要提出具體的例子或細節
5. 不要提出新意見

---

### ✎ Task 1

**請看看這些用來總結論證的固定短語。**

| 總結用的 set-phrases | |
|---|---|
| • In conclusion, 總結來說， | • On balance, 持平來說， |
| • In the last analysis, 歸根結底， | • Overall, it is clear that v.p. 整體而言，很清楚的是 v.p. |
| • To sum up, 總而言之， | • I would recommend that v.p. 我會力薦 v.p. |
| • To summarize, 總結一下， | |

☆ 請使用這些用語來總結你的論證。

☆ 你可以從 Unit 6 的 Task 2 中選用一個表達意見的 set-phrase 來重申你的意見。

☆ 不要使用你在「引言」用過的 set-phrase。請試著用不同的 set-phrase，讓閱卷者知道你懂更多的 set-phrases。

### ✎ Task 2

**請看第 64, 97, 121, 145 頁 Reading 範例文章的結語，注意它們如何遵循上面的 checklist，並使用了 Task 1 中的哪一個 set-phrase。**

- Reading 1 用了 To summarize 和 It is my opinion 。
- Reading 2 用了 In the last analysis。其中並沒有意見固定片語，因為這是「問題／解決方法」的文章。
- Reading 3 用了 In conclusion。其中並沒有意見固定片語，因為這是「問題／解決方法」的文章。
- Reading 4 用了 To sum up 和 I firmly believe that。

☆ 請留意到結語全都偏短且沒有提出任何的新資訊。

---

❌ 錯誤

❖ <u>On</u> conclusion

❖ In <u>a</u> last analysis

❖ To <u>summary</u>

❖ <u>In</u> balance

❖ Overall, <u>it clear</u> that

❖ I <u>will</u> recommend that

---

✔ 正確

❖ <u>In</u> conclusion

❖ In <u>the</u> last analysis

❖ To <u>summarize</u>

❖ <u>On</u> balance

❖ Overall, <u>it is clear</u> that

❖ I <u>would</u> recommend that

---

　　接下來的練習我們將聚焦於 set-phrases 的細節，以確保你已學會正確用法。

## ✏ Task 3

請在空格中各填入一個單字來完成下列句子。

1. (1) _____ summarize, it is my opinion (2)_____ the arts are important for everyone, and the benefits of the state supporting them far outweigh the costs.

2. In (3)_____ last analysis, if we are all going to share this planet in the future, we will need to be less selfish about our desires and expectations.

3. (4)_____ conclusion, cybercrime causes great harm to private citizens and public institutions. Overall, it's clear that both banks and customers have a role to play in preventing it.

4. To sum (5)_____, although social networking sites have brought individuals closer together, they have not had the same effect on society or local communities. I (6)_____ believe that local communities should do more to try and involve local people in local activities in order to promote the future of community life.

解答

1. (1) To  (2) that    2. (3) the    3. (4) In    4. (5) up  (6) do

**Task 4**

請看下列句子，找出 **set-phrases** 裡的錯誤並且修正它們。

1. To summary, it is opinion that the arts are important for everyone, and the benefits of the state supporting them far outweigh the costs.

   → _____

2. In a last analysis, if we are all going to share this planet in the future, we will need to be less selfish about our desires and expectations.

   → _____

3. On conclusion, cybercrime causes great harm to private citizens and public institutions.

   → _____

4. To sum it up, although social networking sites have brought individuals closer together, they have not had the same effect on society or local communities.

   → _____

5. Overall it clear that the benefits outweigh the disadvantages.

   → _____

6. I will recommend that everyone should have one.

   → _____

7. In a last analysis, it's better to be without, than have one that doesn't work properly.

   → _____

8. On balancing, most people said they preferred it.

   → _____

1. To **summarize**, it is **my** opinion that the arts are important for everyone, and the benefits of the state supporting them far outweigh the costs.
   總之，我的意見是，藝術對每個人都重要，由國家支持它們的好處遠遠超過成本。

2. In **the** last analysis, if we are all going to share this planet in the future, we will need to be less selfish about our desires and expectations.
   歸根結底，假如我們未來全都要共享這個星球，我們就需要在慾望和期待上少點私心。

3. **In** conclusion, cybercrime causes great harm to private citizens and public institutions.
   總結來說，網路犯罪會對平民和公共機構造成重大的損害。

4. To sum **it** up, although social networking sites have brought individuals closer together, they have not had the same effect on society or local communities.
   總而言之，雖然社交網站拉近了人與人之間的距離，但對社會或地方社區卻沒有產生相同的效應。

5. Overall, it **is** clear that the benefits outweigh the disadvantages.
   整體而言，利大於弊是顯而易見的。

6. I **would** recommend that everyone should have one.
   我會力薦每個人都該要有一個。

7. In **the** last analysis, it's better to be without, than have one that doesn't work properly.
   歸根結底，與其擁有一個不能正常工作的設備，還不如沒有。

8. On **balance**, most people said they preferred it.
   持平來說，大部分的人都說他們更喜歡這樣。

☆ 務必要學會並準確使用這些 set-phrases。要聚焦於小細節，尤其是小詞、單字的結尾和 set-phrases 的結尾。

　　最後來看一些英文寫作的真題範例。

**Extra Practice Essays**

利用前面學過的重點，練習針對以下題目來寫短文。請聚焦於結語的寫作。

**TOPIC 1** 107 年學士後中醫（義守）

二、作文題（共 **20** 分）：Please write in at least 250 words a well-organized essay to express your opinion on "Chinese Philosophy and Chinese Medicine".

**TOPIC 2** 104 年學士後西醫（高醫）

**IV. Essay Writing: 20 points**

Please write a well-organized essay with at least 200 words to express your opinion on medical malpractice.

"Statistics show that approximately 195,000 people are killed every year by medical errors in the US. Between 15,000 and 19,000 malpractice suits are brought against doctors each year." Are there efficient and practical ways to reduce the rate of medical error? Should doctors be solely responsible for their errors? What sort of legal protection should doctors be entitled to?

在你結束這個單元之前，請將下列的清單看過，確定你能將所有要點都勾選起來。如果有一些要點你還搞不清楚，請回頭再次研讀本單元的相關部分。

☐ 我學到了如何為文章寫結語。

☐ 我學到了一些結語可使用的 set-phrases。

☐ 我學到了在使用 set-phrases 時，所應避免的一些常見錯誤。

☐ 我練習去使用了這些 set-phrases。

☐ 我看到了一些真題範例，並針對那些題目練習寫了文章。

UNIT
**15**

Notes

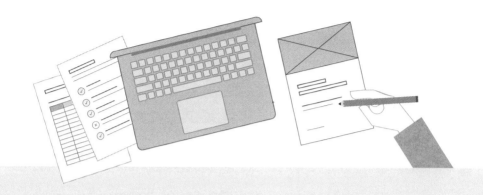

# Appendices／附錄

## 後醫英文寫作批改範例

在本書最後，附上幾篇我在指導學生準備後醫英文寫作時的
實際範例，你可以參考看看別人寫的作文及我的批改和評
析，並反思自己在寫作時是否也常會犯相同的錯誤。

# Sample Essays 1

Obesity is a global problem, especially in the developed world. What are the causes of this problem, and how can Western Medicine solve it? Write 250 words (4 paragraphs).

✏️ 學員作文 & 校正範例

建議分數：5~10

**❶**Obesity is a civilized illness that ~~leading~~ (s) to many critical diseases, such as

cardiovascular

~~cradiovascular~~ diseases and diabetes. **❷**This issue ~~haunted~~ (s) people all over the

ies

world, especially in **❸**the developed ~~country~~.

a variety of

There are ~~variaty~~ causes of this annoying problem. First of all, eating habit is

resulting

the most direct factor ~~result~~ in obesity. **❹**People who ~~lived~~ in a fast-paced

society often neglect their health because of the stress to catch up with others.

Getting too much pressure from life, many people choose to soothe their soul by

overeating. Furthermore, the lifestyle of these people is **❺**another factor that

gives          ↓being

~~give~~ rise to overweight. Instead of spending leisure time to exercise, they bury

themselves into their every day tasks. Even worse, some people stay up all night

to finish their jobs. Due to sleep deprivation and physical inactivity, the risk of

gaining weight is dramatically rising.

Fortunately, Western Medicine is able to control ~~overweight~~ [obesity] and even more, prevent people from suffering from it. In a short-term fix, medicine and surgery may be an effective option to help people treat their weight by inhibiting their appetite. However, they may regain their weight back if they do not eat and exercise properly. In a long-term fix, appropriate diet habits and regular activities are the simplest way to maintain one's body weight. Moreover, precision medicine, a brand new type of medication, can provide a personalized treatment by analyzing ~~pateints'~~ [patients'] gene of high risk of obesity. Personalized medicine along with adequate diet and exercise can lower the risk of people who may suffer from obesity.

In conclusion, though obesity is difficult to treat and has a high relapse rate, advanced medical treatments increase chances for people to live in a healthier lifestyle.

## 綜合評析

**Strengths**

你的英文很好。你對這個話題有一些很不錯的想法,並且把它們清晰而有邏輯地表達出來了。

**Weaknesses**

① 誤 Obesity is a civilized illness that leading to many critical diseases…
　　→ 此句沒有主要動詞。每個句子都必須有一個主要動詞。
　 正 **Obesity is a civilized illness that leads to many critical diseases…**

② 誤 ... This issue haunted people....

    → 動詞時態錯誤。在這裡你不應該使用過去簡單式，而應該使用現在簡單式，因為它是與時間無關的「事實」。

  正 **... This issue haunts people....**

---

③ 誤 ... the developed country.

    → 請記得在必要時應使用複數名詞。

  正 **... the developed countries.**

---

④ 誤 ... People who lived in a fast-paced society....

    → 動詞時態錯誤。與前面一樣，這裡只是在說明一個與時間無關的事實，所以用現在簡單式就可以了。

  正 **... People who live in a fast-paced society....**

---

⑤ 誤 ... another factor that give rise to....

    → 主詞是第三人稱，記得在動詞後面加 s。

  正 **... another factor that gives rise to....**

---

### Learn this language

- **a variety of Xs**（必須接複數名詞）
- **be overweight**（overweight 是形容詞，所以在此文中應使用名詞的 obesity）
- **regain s/th = get s/th back**（~~regain s/th back~~ 是錯誤的用法）

# Sample Essays 2

Many patients' families find a family member's illness adds to their stress and pressure. What can doctors and hospital managers do to help patients' families deal with the stress of having a sick family member?
**Please write a well organized essay in at least 250 words (3 paragraphs) explaining what you think.**

📝 學員作文 & 校正範例

建議分數：11~15

Taking care of a patient is an affliction for most of the patients' families, especially the one who has been bedridden for years ❶may ~~let~~ their caregivers [give] ~~under~~ too much pressure. ❷As ~~a~~ health care practitioners, it may be difficult for us to understand how much stress the patients' families are facing~~, with,~~ ❸~~however~~, [However] we can reach our hands to them before they fall into the abyss of despair.

In general, ❹the origins of the pressure ~~are~~ come from financial problem and the shortage of caregivers. Therefore, the first step we should take is listening to patients' families concerns. Understanding what torment they are in is the most vital thing for giving them the help they need. After that, we can provide them [with] ↓ some information and ~~sources~~ [resources] that may help them overcome the difficulties. For instance, the **❺** ~~socail~~ welfare system ~~from the government~~ provides various

[annotation above: government social]

kinds of financial subsidies and services for long-term care requesters. **❻**Not

only ~~did~~ the system alleviate the financial situation but **❼**also ~~improve~~ the

[annotation above "did": does] [annotation above "also": ↓ it improves]

quality of care. Last but not least, we can set up a sense of belongings~~ ~~for the

families. It is pivotal for them to aware that there are some shoulders which they

[annotation above: be ↓]

can always lean on and help them ~~getting~~ through all the ordeals.

In conclusion, supporting the patients' families is as ~~impotant~~ as treating **❽**~~a~~

[annotation above "impotant": important] [annotation above "a": an]

~~illness~~ patient. A wonderful medical team is a group that everyone in it can

receive the supports~~ ~~they need. Once the caregivers are able to ameliorate the

stress they have, the patients will get better care and treatments.

---

## 綜合評析

**Strengths**

你的英文很好。你在句型結構方面運用得很廣且動詞時態的使用整體來說是正確的。你對這個議題有一些很不錯的想法,並且把它們表達得清晰而有邏輯。

**Weaknesses**

① 誤 … may let their caregivers under too much pressure.

　　→ 此句沒有什麼意義。

　正 **… may give their caregivers too much pressure.**

....................................................................................

② 誤 As a health care practitioners….

　　→ 注意此處的名詞是複數,不可以加冠詞 a。

　正 **As health care practitioners….**

....................................................................................

③ 當使用 "However" 時，你必須開始一個新的句子，因為這是一個新的想法。

→ 一句話 = 一個想法，一個想法 = 一句話。

④ 誤 … the origins of the pressure are come from financial problem….

→ come from 前不可以再用 be 動詞。

正 **… the origins of the pressure come from financial problem….**

⑤ 誤 … social welfare system from the government….

→ 搭配詞的使用可讓你的寫作看起來更高級。

正 **… government social welfare system….**

⑥ 誤 … Not only did the system alleviate….

→ 動詞時態錯誤。在這裡你不應該使用過去簡單式，而應該使用現在簡單式，因為它是與時間無關的「事實」。

正 **… Not only does the system alleviate….**

⑦ 誤 … also improve the quality of care….

→ 動詞 improve 沒有主詞，必須加上第三人稱主詞 it。

正 **… also it improves the quality of care….**

⑧ 誤 … a illness patient.

→ 請確認在以母音開頭的名詞之前，冠詞要用 an，且 patient 前應用形容詞 ill。

正 **… an ill patient.**

**Learn this language**

- **face s/th** 或 **be faced with s/th** 都是正確用法，但是 ~~face with s/th~~ 是錯的。
- **provide s/o with s/th**（表示提供某樣東西給某人）
- **sources** 是指來源、起源（= origins）；**resources** 則是指資源（= things you can use）
- **a sense of belonging** 是「歸屬感」，不可寫成 ~~a sense of belongings~~。
- **be aware that v.p.**
- **help s/o to V** 是幫助、幫忙，不可用 ~~help s/o Ving~~。
- **illness** (*n.*)、**ill** (*adj.*) 使用時要留意。

# Sample Essays 3

Stress related illness is the number one killer in the world today. What can people do to reduce the impact of stress? **Please write in at least 200 words (3 paragraphs) a well organized essay to express your opinion.**

✏️ 學員作文＆校正範例

建議分數：11~15

People in modern society always live a fast-paced life. Because of the development of the Internet, they continue to receive stimulation from the virtual world after work, and ❶this ~~make~~ makes it difficult to relax truly. It is precisely ❷because ~~of~~ people are often ~~be~~ tense that the pressure accumulates over the years, and it is easy for people to suffer from stress-related diseases, such as bipolar disorder and depression. ~~people~~ People are often in a state of tension, the pressure builds up over time, ❸easily ~~cause~~ causing people to suffer from stress-related diseases, such as bipolar disorder and depression. Therefore, in order to avoid this situation, learning how to reduce the impact of stress has become an important issue.

First of all, people should clarify the source of their stress. If it is caused by interpersonal stress, people should try to solve the problem through communication; if it comes from work or academic load, people must try to take time out of busy things. The researches ~~show~~ [shows] that ❹~~find~~ [finding] some ways to help oneself release stress can keep people ~~the motivation~~ [motivated] for progress. Example of these methods are as follows: First, meditation. Studies show that the human body's breathing, blood pressure, and brain secretions will be maintained in the most peaceful state ❺when people ~~with~~ [have] stable breathing and dismissing distracting thoughts, and ❻~~it~~ [they] will be able to fight depression. Second, exercise regularly. Exercise can promote the brain [to] release endorphin, a substance that makes people feel happy, and exercise can also accelerate metabolism, relax the body and reduce mental stress. Third, listen to music. When people are under tension, music can relax the tense nervous system and relieve the stress.

However, in addition to the above methods, there are many ways to relieve emotions. No matter what ~~to~~ [you] do, the most important thing is to find the most comfortable way to truly achieve the purpose of reducing stress and making yourself [have] a happier life.

---

### 綜合評析

**Strengths**

你在句型結構方面運用得很廣且動詞時態的使用整體來說是正確的。你對這個議題有一些很不錯的想法，而且論述清晰有條理。

① 誤 … this make it difficult to relax truly….

→ 主詞是第三人稱時，動詞要加 s。另外要注意，truly 修飾動詞時應置於動詞之前。

正 **… this makes it difficult to truly relax….**

② 誤 … because of people are often be tense….

→ because of 後面不可接 v.p.，應該改用 because v.p.。此外，句子中不可同時有兩個動詞。

正 **… because people are often tense….**

③ 誤 … easily cause people to suffer….

→ 此處的 cause 必須改成 Ving，因為你正在描述結果。

正 **… easily causing people to suffer….**

④ 誤 … find some ways to help oneself release stress can keep….

→ 在此句中動詞 can 的主詞是 find，但是動詞不能當主詞，應該改為 Ving 或 n.p.。

正 **… finding some ways to help oneself release stress can keep….**

⑤ 誤 … when people with stable breathing and dismissing distracting thoughts

→ 在 when 之後必須接 v.p.。

正 **… when people have stable breathing and dismiss distracting thoughts**

⑥ 誤 … it will be able to fight depression….

→ 你應該使用代名詞 they 來代指句子前面的 "people"。

正 **… they will be able to fight depression….**

**Learn this language**

• 「研究顯示」的正確說法是 **The research shows**，要注意不能用 ~~The researches show~~，因為 **research** 泛指「研究」時是不可數名詞。

• **promote s/th to V**（促進某事物……）

• **make o/self V**（使某人……）

# Sample Essays 4

Young people today have more opportunities than any other generation before, from longer life spans and better medical care, to better education and more freedom of information and expression. What are some of the best things about being young in Taiwan? **Write 250 words (3 paragraphs)**.

📝 學員作文＆校正範例

建議分數：6~10

Young people today have better education, medical care, and longer average life span than our predecessors. However, as a young person in Taiwan, I think there are other better things besides all of the above benefits.

Taiwan is located in an important strategic position in East Asia, and is rich in various natural resources. ❶According to Portuguese who passed by hundreds of years ago, "Ilha Formosa!" you can know how beautiful Taiwan is.*(no meaning )*

Because
❷~~It is also because~~ of rich natural resources and location in the main traffic arteries, Taiwan has become a hotly contested spot for hundreds of years, which created a rich humanities history. ❸We ~~had~~ learned Taiwan's history since we

were                                    homeland                              every
~~are~~ young, to understand our ~~hometown~~ better, and to understand that not ~~ever~~ thing can succeed at the first try, but through the efforts of the predecessors for a long time. Just like freedom and democracy. ❹All of this is irrelevant to the

topic of the essay. The ancestors formed groups to fight for the right to vote, or

through many resistances against the totalitarian government, can we have

common suffrage now. [above "common": universal] And the same-sex marriages adopted in recent years

have guaranteed that people of the same sex can have the right to marry. It is

also achieved through decades of ancestors' initiatives and petitions, as well as

constant dialogue with the society.

In Taiwan, many social issues are constantly being discussed every day. **❶People**

**with different political inclinations** [above: are] **also arguing every day.** However, everyone

knows that everything is hard to come by, so they still tolerate each other's

opinion, and all voices can be heard, which can create more sparks between

opinions. I think that the best things about being young in Taiwan, is that we can

learn how to express and accept ideas without intervention (*no meaning*), and

become more tolerant and wise.

---

### 綜合評析

**Strengths**

你的文法使用整體來說是正確的,句型多樣化,用詞也恰當。

**Weaknesses**

① 你的文章大部分內容都沒有回答這個問題,也就是說,你寫的大部分內容與主
題根本不相關,所以你的分數會較低。寫作時請務必確認你寫的內容沒有離
題,並不要寫與主題無關的多餘字句。

② 誤 … It is also because of rich natural resources and location in the main traffic arteries, Taiwan has become a hotly contested spot for hundreds of years,….

→ 不要用 It is also。

正 **… Because of rich natural resources and location in the main traffic arteries, Taiwan has become a hotly contested spot for hundreds of years,….**

③ 誤 … We had learned Taiwan's history since we are young

→ 不要在你的文章中使用過去完成式。在此使用過去簡單式即可,因為你只是在寫一段已經結束的時間。

正 **… We learned Taiwan's history since we were young**

④ 誤 … People with different political inclinations also arguing every day.

→ 這個句子中沒有助動詞。

正 **… People with different political inclinations are also arguing every day.**

## Learn this language

- 提到「故鄉」時,因為台灣是國家而不是一個城鎮,所以不能用 hometown,應該說 Taiwan is my **homeland**。或是說 Taipei is my hometown。
- 「普選權」的說法是 **universal suffrage**。(~~common suffrage~~)

# Sample Essays 5

Obesity is a global problem, especially in the developed world. What are the causes of this problem, and how can Western Medicine solve it?
**Write 250 words (4 paragraphs).**

✏️ 學員作文＆校正範例

建議分數：6~10

**❶**Obesity, the notorious mastermind (*no meaning*), ~~have been triggering~~ <sup>triggers</sup> many

other health issues and ~~have been claiming~~ <sup>claims</sup> people's ~~life~~ <sup>lives</sup> even before they are not

conscious about **❷**how serious their condition ~~are~~ <sup>is</sup>. The main reason that people

nowadays are getting fatter and fatter can be summarized as the following

aspects- the change in the lifestyle, the preponderance of fast food restaurants

and gastronomy. All in all, people in the modern society are facing stacks of

pressure, **❸**which ~~prompt as~~ <sup>prompts us</sup> to pursue hasty lifestyle and sedentary life style in

which we put much less pressure on exercise (*no meaning*). With a view to

settling the problem (*no meaning*), there are obesity clinics available in every

hospitals, in which people can appeal to (*no meaning*) appropriate procedures

and consultants to cut their weights (*no meaning*). In the following paragraphs, I

will elaborate on how and what kind of ~~measurements~~ <sup>measures</sup> can be adopted

~~in the aspect of~~ <sup>by</sup> western medicine.

[4]If you ~~are~~ unfortunately ~~becomes~~ corpulent and are at loss about

losing weight
~~cutting your weights down~~, then please have a look ~~on~~ [at] the following

information. Generally speaking, there are obesity clinics accessible in [5]every

hospitals, in which ~~consist of the dietician~~ [there are] doctors who are specialists in weight

loss. They ~~not only~~ [will] help you understand how [6]our body ~~metabolise~~ [metabolises] and give

you professional guidelines. If it needs ~~be~~ , they can also tailor the weight loss

plan for you. If you really have made up your mind in weight loss, it makes no

reason for you to skip the resource. (*no meaning*)


In addition to the aforementioned resource, there are also behavior ~~consolers~~ [counselors]

and supporting groups where many peers can ~~cut~~ [lose] weight with you and reinforce

the obligation to keep up the plan. What's more, upon seeing other people

succeed in getting their weights down, a sense of incumbency comes over you

(*no meaning*) and [7]~~prop~~ [props] up your confidence in achieving the following plans.

~~Granted that~~ [If] the above ~~measurements~~ [measures] really don't work, you still can adopt

intrusive medical treatment which ~~inclusive of the excision of the partial~~ [includes the partial of excision the]

stomach and some prescribed medicine to block fat absorbance.


With so many treatments available, I see no reason that you avert yourself from

facing the fact (*no meaning*). After all , if you were not to face the facts and

begin to cut your weight, you might pay even heavier price and even fall victims

<u>to the assassinators</u> (*no meaning*) that prevails all over the world.

## 綜合評析

**Strengths**

你的英文還不錯。你在句型結構方面運用得很廣且動詞時態的使用整體來說是正確的。

**Weaknesses**

① 誤 Obesity, the notorious mastermind, have been triggering

→ 不要在你的文章中使用隱喻。你的英文必須極為優異才可能使用適當地隱喻，而你的英文程度還達不到。此外，使用了太多無實際意義卻常被錯誤使用的花俏詞彙是你的一大問題，而且你在非常基本的英語語法規則也犯了很多錯誤。建議你寫作時將精力集中在簡單、清晰和準確的用語上，避免花俏的詞彙和難懂的想法。

→ 在這句中，您的數字和動詞時態也用得不正確。此處使用現在簡單式即可，因為你描述的是一個與時間無關的事實，另外，注意主詞和動詞的單複數須一致。

正 **obesity triggers....**

② 誤 ... how serious their condition are.

→ 注意主詞和動詞的單複數須一致。

正 **... how serious their condition is.**

③ 誤 ... which prompt....

→ 注意，當主詞為第三人稱單數時，動詞一定要加 s。

正 **... which prompts....**

④ 誤 ... If you are unfortunately becomes corpulent....

→ 務必留意句子中主詞和動詞的一致性，不可以在一個句子中同時出現 be 動詞和 become。

正 **... If you unfortunately become corpulent....**

⑤ 誤 ... every hospitals....

→ 在 every 之後應使用單數名詞。

正 **... every hospital....**

⑥ 誤 ... our body metabolise....

→ 當主詞為第三人稱單數時，動詞一定要加 s。

正 **... our body metabolises....**

---

⑦ 誤 ... prop up your confidence....

→ 當主詞為第三人稱單數時，動詞一定要加 s。

正 **... props up your confidence....**

---

## Learn this language

• **life** 指一人的生命。指多人的生命時，要用複數形 **lives**。
• 「解決問題」是 **solving the problem**。（~~settling the problem~~）
• 「減重、減肥」是 **lose weight**。（~~cut their weights, cut their weights down, cut weight~~）
• **look at** 是「請看……」；**look on** 是「旁觀、觀望」
• 「顧問」是 **counselors**，不可拼成 ~~consolers~~。
• **measures** = methods of doing something 對策、措施
  **measurements** = how long something is 測量值

# Sample Essays 6

Young people today have more opportunities than any other generation before, from longer life spans and better medical care, to better education and more freedom of information and expression. What are some of the best things about being young in Taiwan? **Write 250 words (3 paragraphs).**

學員作文 & 校正範例

建議分數：11~15

With the progress of the times and the development of various industries, humans live and enjoy better and peaceful lives than any other generation before. ~~Advenced~~ Advanced technologies bring convenience and comfort to every aspects of our ~~livings~~ lives.

~~Speak~~ Speaking of best things about being young in Taiwan. ~~Two~~ , two advantages that I consider to be critical ~~of several~~ are the medical care and the ~~mutipul~~ multiple options of education. In the field of medicine in Taiwan, no matter eastern or western medicine, ~~aboudant~~ abundant and strong resources that support the research and development of medicine, lead to the effective and convenient medical care nowadays. ❶The earlier that disease ~~be~~ is found and cured, the less pain and better ~~recover~~ recovery that children ~~could~~ will have. What's even better is the National Health Insurance. The benevolent and kind policy brings health not only to normal

182

citizens but also to the people in the <u>dilemma of economy</u> (*no meaning*).

Another good thing of being young in Taiwan to me is the various ways to

accept education

~~acepet~~ educa~~i~~tion. Different industries mean the requirements of human

fields              education

resources from ❷<u>different ~~field~~</u>. ❸<u>Multiple ↓options ~~of the education~~</u> help young

interested           , which

students to discover the fields that they are in~~x~~terested in and love~~,~~ ❹~~Which~~

makes them keep the passion and energy of learning a~~nd~~ in order to choose the

truly

job that they ~~turly~~ love in the future.


In conclusion, the reason that I consider medical care and education to be two of

important

best things about being young in Taiwan, is that the most ~~inportant~~ thing of all is

health                    healthy

~~healh~~. ❺<u>And only if students are ~~healty~~ that they might learned and grow with</u>

<u>joy.</u> (*no meaning*) In the future, they will be talented and strong to bring the

industry

continuous development of ❻<u>every ~~industries~~</u> that people could live better lives.


---

### 🗒 綜合評析

**Strengths**

你的英文很好。在句型結構方面運用得很廣且動詞時態的使用整體來說是正確
的。對議題有一些還不錯的想法,並能有條理的表達出來。


**Weaknesses**

① 誤 The earlier that disease be found….

    → 句子少了主要的動詞。

  正 **The earlier that disease is found…**

② 誤 ... different field....

→ 請注意名詞的單複數使用時機。此處因為 different，所以應該使用複數。

正 **... different fields**

---

③ 誤 Multiple options of the education....

→ 善用字詞搭配可以讓寫出來的文句更自然、更高級。

正 **Multiple education options....**

---

④ 誤 Which makes them keep the passion....

→ 除非是疑問句，否則不能以 Which 為開頭。

---

⑤ 誤 And only if students are healthy that they might learned and grow with joy....

→ 這句話的邏輯是錯誤的。請將你的句子與下方句子進行比較，看看有什麼不同。另外，要注意動詞時態，因為你談論的是與時間無關的事實，所以應該使用現在簡單式。

正 **Students might learn and grow with joy only if they are healthy.**

---

⑥ 誤 ... every industries....

→ every 後面應該加單數名詞。

正 **... every industry....**

---

⑦ 在這篇文章中出現了許多拼字方面的錯誤，請特別留意！

# Sample Essays 7

Many patients' families find a family member's illness adds to their stress and pressure. What can doctors and hospital managers do to help patients' families deal with the stress of having a sick family member?
**Please write a well organized essay in at least 250 words (3 paragraphs) explaining what you think.**

## 學員作文＆校正範例

建議分數：6~10

With the development of the aging population in our society, it is needless to say that doctors in this generation are facing more and more stress. Speaking of the condition in which patients are severely ill, the responsibility of the doctors goes far beyond than just prescribing medicine. Trapped in the dire straight in their life, what [1]they needs is emotional support in addition to the physical treatment. In the following paragraph, I will raise the example of my grandma, who had been properly treated both physically and emotionally by the doctor.

give                    on                                    to deal
Moreover I will ~~raise~~ my opinion ~~in~~ how to face and [2]help patients ~~in dealing with~~ the bottleneck (*no meaning*) in their life.

[3]Although my grandma had passed away about one year ago because of the metastasis of the leiomyosarcoma, a malicious cancer in which patients often

live less than one year according to the prognosis, I am glad and sincerely

grateful to ❹the visiting doctor who ~~have given~~ *gave* both appropriate and prompt

treatment to my grandma. ❺Had it not *been* for him, my grandma would not *have* lived up

to more than six years suffering from this type of cancer. As the visiting doctor,

❻he not only ~~arrange~~ *arranged* suitable examination to keep the metastasis at bay but also

❻~~conduct~~ *conducted* surgery promptly and precisely upon discovering new metastasis sites.

Much to our relief, ❻he always ~~give~~ *gave* us the detailed analysis ~~in~~ *of* both the

condition and the option of treatments which we ought to take to give the

highest life quality to my grandma <u>even in condition of the illness</u> (*redundant*).

As to us, it serves as the <u>light house</u> (*no meaning*) when the condition is

desperate to us.


In my opinion, a good doctor should ~~own~~ *have* the following features. First and fore

most , he or she should give the detailed and understandable description and

analysis according to the actual condition to both the families and the patient. In

this condition, he must be empathetic to the patients and treat ~~him~~ *them* as if ~~he~~ *they* were

his family. Second, he must take the responsibility in every treatment conducted

and ~~advise~~ *advice* given by him. Last but not least, they should give emotional support

because sometimes the encouragement may prop up the patients and their

families.

## Strengths

你的英文還不錯，對此議題也有一些還不錯的想法。

## Weaknesses

你的介紹很混亂，看起來好像你要寫的是醫生面臨的壓力，但題目是要寫家庭成員的壓力。請確保你寫的內容與題意相符。

① 誤 … they needs….
→ 主詞與動詞須一致。
正 **… they need….**

② 誤 …help patients is dealing with….
→ help s/o to V
正 **… help patients to deal with**

第二段是對你生活中曾經發生的事情做描述，這些事情發生在過去的時間，所以這一段中所有的動詞都應該用過去式。

③ 誤 Although my grandma had passed away about one year ago….
→ 不要在你的文章中使用過去完成式，使用過去簡單式即可。
正 **Although my grandma passed away about one year ago….**

④ 誤 … the visiting doctor who have given both appropriate and prompt treatment….
→ 動詞時態錯誤。這裡應該使用過去式描述已經結束的事。
正 **… the visiting doctor who gave both appropriate and prompt treatment….**

⑤ 誤 Had it not for him….
正 **Had it not been for him**

⑥ 誤 … he not only arrange….
… conduct surgery promptly….

... he always give us....

→ 動詞時態錯誤，應使用過去式。

正 ... he not only arranged....

... conducted surgery promptly....

... he always gave us....

## Learn this language

- **give an opinion on s/th**「對某事發表意見」。(~~raise an opinion in s/th~~)
- **analysis of s/th**「對某事的分析」。(~~analysis in s/th~~)
- **advise** (*v.*) **/ advice** (*n.*)，使用時別搞混了。

Notes

國家圖書館出版品預行編目資料

論證型英文寫作速成教戰 / Quentin Brand作. -- 初版. --
臺北市：波斯納出版有限公司, 2023.07
　　面： 公分

　ISBN: 978-626-97353-0-3（平裝）

　1. CST: 英語　2. CST: 寫作法

805.17　　　　　　　　　　　　　　112005823

# 論證型英文寫作速成教戰

作　　者／Quentin Brand
執行編輯／朱曉瑩

出　　版／波斯納出版有限公司
地　　址／台北市 100 館前路 26 號 6 樓
電　　話／(02) 2314-2525
傳　　真／(02) 2312-3535
客服專線／(02) 2314-3535
客服信箱／btservice@betamedia.com.tw
郵撥帳號／19493777
帳戶名稱／波斯納出版有限公司

總 經 銷／時報文化出版企業股份有限公司
地　　址／桃園市龜山區萬壽路二段 351 號
電　　話／(02) 2306-6842

出版日期／2023 年 7 月初版一刷
定　　價／360 元
I S B N／978-626-97353-0-3

貝塔網址：www.betamedia.com.tw

喚醒你的英文語感！

Get a Feel for English !

喚醒你的英文語感！

Get a Feel for English !

喚醒你的英文語感！

Get a Feel for English !